Tuesday

*Rhianna
Thank you so much
for all your work, you star!
Love Jo xx*

By

Jo R. Brown

For Tára,

Thank you for being an absolute star!

About the author:

Jo R. Brown is an English author of contemporary fiction.

Jo grew up in the West Country, notably Bath. She now lives in Gloucestershire with her husband, two (grown up) wonderful children and one characterful tortoiseshell cat.

Her first novel Helter Skelter is also available on Amazon to rave reviews.

Chapter one

The day seemed as any other day; just an average Tuesday. The only unusual thing about today was that I had the day off work and was meeting Charley for coffee.

I was really looking forward to catching up with her; our busy schedules meant that meeting up had become a logistical nightmare. Charley was a reporter and had just returned from a trip to Venice (lucky thing), so had a free day. Venice is one of my most favourite places in the world. I could quite happily live out the rest of my days there: the light, the colours, the magic and the mystery. As I had no way or plans to go there any time soon, hearing Charley's stories would have to do for the time being.

As it was my day off, I got up later than usual. Sitting in my dressing gown on the sofa with a cup of coffee in my hand, I switched on the news on the TV. It was the weather, I just love listening to the weather forecast, I don't know why, I love hearing the shipping forecast too! I don't even have a boat, or know anyone with a boat, let alone anyone who goes fishing, but there is something strangely comforting and reassuring about these forecasts.

All of a sudden there was an almighty 'boom' outside my window. I nearly dropped my coffee. Abruptly distracted from the routine weather update, I got up and rushed to the window to see what had happened.

Outside I could see a big crash between what looked like a lorry and a small car. There were lots of people running to the scene of the accident. I hesitated, *do I ring 999*, or had someone already done that? I couldn't go down, I wasn't dressed, besides there seemed to be crowd there already and I'd only get in the way. Sure enough within a few minutes the sirens and blue lights arrived.

Smoke started to appear from under the car, I closed the window so it didn't get into the flat. I wanted to leave the view and get dressed, but morbid curiosity got the better of me. I watched as the police tried to get the crowd to move back and let the fire and ambulance crews help out the casualties. Things weren't looking too good, from what I could see they dragged a man from the lorry, he seemed to be unconscious. The firemen were at the car with cutters trying to gain access to the victim, I guess.

An ambulance quickly drove off with the lorry driver inside, but there seemed to be a problem getting in to the car. *Jeez, I hope they get in there soon, poor person,* I thought to myself. Suddenly a lot of activity happened; they managed to gain access to the car – incredibly a young man then pulled himself out of the car and began staggering. Quickly a paramedic grabbed hold of him for support. A few seconds later, another boom, and the car burst into a huge fireball.

What the heck! I instinctively jumped back from the window and drew the curtains closed, afraid the glass might blow. Luckily it stayed intact. I sat momentarily back down on the sofa, questioning what I should do. Was I in danger, should I phone a friend, leave, find the cat? Oh wait, I didn't have a cat! I decided that I was probably in a state of mild shock, and having a glass of brandy was the sensible thing to do. I didn't have any brandy.

Having sat down for a few minutes, I felt recomposed and cautiously returned to the window. I drew back the curtain, the glass in the window was fine, just a little blackened. The fireball had died down and the firemen seemed to have the situation under control. There was still a lot of smoke in the air and it was difficult to make anything out at ground level, it was all very chaotic. The crowds had gone, probably made a run for it, if they'd had any sense. There were now three fire engines and a couple of police cars, but the ambulances had left.

Even though the window was closed the smell of burning rubber had seeped into the room. It was a sickening stench. Feeling a bit dazed and confused, I thought the best course of action was to get up. Tentatively I had a very quick shower: I wasn't very comfortable in the shower cubicle, feeling naked and vulnerable. Dry and clean, I got dressed without thinking. I didn't feel like applying any make-up, I could just about focus on brushing my teeth.

I took one last look out of the window before leaving the flat. There was still a commotion going on outside. I really felt it was time to leave the flat, the street, in fact the whole area, a change of scene was definitely required. Going down the communal stairs I could hear the shouts and sounds of the burning car getting significantly louder as I got closer to street level. Also the smell was penetrating

3

the hallway, much stronger than in my flat. Luckily there was a rear entrance to the building so I didn't have to go past the wreckage. I opened the back door and as I did the sun shone brightly in my face. I looked up at the sky, it was pale blue and clear. Outside the back door was a long thin 'garden' - *I use that word cautiously it's more like a neglected strip of wasteland* - with an overgrown path running along the side all the way to the end, where a gate stands. There was no sign of the devastation that was going on outside the front of the building, apart from the awful smell of burning rubber hanging in the air. I walked briskly to the end of the garden and out of the gate into the alley which ran along the end of the gardens.

Dodging the bins, and other debris which lined the alley, I emerged onto a quiet side street. Phew, I started to feel a little more relaxed. *What the hell just happened?* I'm sure I said out loud to myself. As I walked in the opposite direction to the accident, *I'd seen enough thank you,* people were still hurriedly passing me in the direction of the scene to see what was going on. I took a cautious look behind me and could see a plume of grey smoke rising behind my building. I needed to get a long way away, it all seemed much too close for my liking, not to mention those poor guys who were actually involved. How were they? I just hoped they were both ok, what more could I do?

It was relatively early in the morning, but I needed something to calm my nerves. I still had the idea of a brandy in my head. There was a pub on the next corner. I'd make my way there. When I got in everyone was talking about the accident. Having bought my much-needed drink, I sat down at a table and texted Charley, updating her on the morning's unexpected events. She texted straight back saying she'd come and meet me as soon as she could get there.

"I saw it happen," I overheard someone saying. "He just drove straight into him, it was like he just didn't see him," they continued.
"I know, I thought the same, I could see it was about to happen, he came around the corner so fast."
"Terrible, that poor lad. He was lucky to get out alive," and so it continued.

I wanted to listen, somehow hearing people talk about it reassured me that the accident had actually happened, and I hadn't imagined the whole scene. But I didn't want to participate in the discussion, simply listening was just fine by me. I would drink my brandy and wait for Charley to arrive, and just hope that no other incident would occur before then. I was a little shaky you know, I'd only been watching the weather forecast!

Chapter two

It was only about twenty minutes before Charley arrived, but it seemed three times as long. When she walked into the pub I stood up, she came over to me and I immediately started sobbing, it was an impulsive reaction. Charley put her arm around me comfortingly. I felt much better, a good cry really helps sometimes.

"Jeez, what a way to start the day!" I exclaimed.
"Not ideal," Charley replied. "How are you feeling now?"
"Still a bit shaky, but ok. Don't know why I'm so upset, nothing happened to me."
"Well, no, you didn't just get rammed by a huge vehicle, but you did witness it, it's not surprising you feel shaky. Drink up your brandy, let's get outside – it's a beautiful day out there," she said smiling reassuringly.

Charley's words were comforting. I finished off my drink and we left the pub. All the gossipers were still talking about the accident, I guess they will be for years to come too.

"Retail therapy?" Charley suggested.
"Perfect." Heading off to the High Street I started to think about happier things. "Tell me about Venice, oh how I love Venice."
"It was great, oh and I met this gorgeous guy," Charley started to giggle.
"Ooh, do tell me more!" I replied. Charley's love life was always so much more interesting than my own, on account of which mine was non-existent and had been for longer than I care to divulge.

"Well, I was doing a report on the impact of water traffic on the structure of the Venetian buildings – fascinating stuff by the way, you need to read the article, you'll find it so interesting – and I met Tom, yes that's his name, while doing some research. He was very active in campaigning against the huge cruise ships that sail around the city because of their environmental legacy. Turns out that he spent some time living in Venice and is passionate about its preservation. He had studied the effects intensively and written various reports."

"Ooh, he sounds great, just your type," I winked at Charley. She responded by giving out a little squeak of excitement.

"I know, he was just gorgeous too," she continued excitedly. "Anyhow, after we were introduced he sort of looked after me, showed me the parts of Venice tourists don't normally get to see, 'the real Venice'. We got on really well, and I fancied the pants off him…"

"I'm sensing a 'but'?"

"Hmm, well, I'm just not sure he felt the same way about me really. Nothing happened, we just spent some really great days together. It was quite romantic, in a platonic kinda way."

"Oh, platonic. How boring!" I replied, disappointedly.

"Yeah, I know, sucks doesn't it? Seems he isn't 'available', has a girlfriend back home."

"Oh dear, where abouts is home?" I asked.

"You know what, he didn't say. Seriously we really didn't talk about home at all. We were so absorbed in discussing the Venetian environment that nothing outside of Venice really came into the conversation." Charley paused thoughtfully. "I hadn't thought about that until now."

"So you have no contact for him?" I asked.

"I do have his mobile number," Charley replied, "but it doesn't seem appropriate to contact him somehow."

"Venice, the romance that never was…I can see it in the headlines now."

"Oh don't tease Dandie, it's not fair. I thought he was gorgeous, still I guess the gorgeous ones are always taken, eh?"

"Oh no, please don't say that Charley, I need something to hope for." With that we linked arms and giggled down the High Street, we had important shopping to do.

After shopping we grabbed some food and I listened, admittedly with a tinge of envy, all about Charley's travels and adventures; even if they were only platonic, it was a damn sight more interesting and exciting than my life. It seemed Charley and Tom had spent most days together surveying the waterways and traffic, collecting local stories and official data, reflecting on the tourism versus environment issue which inevitably clashed, and generally getting along famously. Dream location, dream man - dream on. Maybe something would develop, maybe he'll return to his girlfriend and find he can't stop thinking about Charley and they will be reunited? Anyhow, back in the real world…

Time was getting on; Charley had writing to do, and I figured I should make my way back home. I really didn't fancy returning to the flat. Who knows what I'd find going on outside in the street.

"Will you be ok?" Charley asked as we prepared to go our separate ways.

"I guess," I replied reluctantly. I could quite easily have listened to Charley's Venetian ramblings for hours, but I knew she had to get on. We said our goodbyes and I thanked her hugely for meeting up with me and providing a much needed and pleasant distraction. Joking that she should expect a call from Venetian Tom, she laughed and headed off down the road. I walked past a travel agent and found myself drawn inside looking at brochures of Venice.

"Did you hear about the crash this morning on Brook Street?" a lady inside asked her companion. I was getting bored of the topic now and took that as my cue to leave the premises, and my dreams of visiting Venice.

I stepped out of the shop onto the pavement.

"Dandelion!" I heard someone shout my name. I turned around to see Jake waving his arms at me.

"Yay, Jake! Just the tonic I need to cheer me up."

"Haha, I'm glad I cheer someone up. What are you up to?"

"Have the day off," I replied.

"Ooh, have you been doing anything exciting?"

"Only witnessing car crashes and dreaming of Venice."

"Cool," Jake hesitated. "...car crashes?"

"Well, just the one thankfully, don't really want to talk about it, but let's just say I prefer an uneventful wake-up call!"

"I'm on my lunch break, d'you fancy a coffee?" Jake asked. I agreed, welcome of any distraction. Any plans I did have for the day had gone to pot anyway.

Jake was a lovely man, a really good friend; he had fair hair which he wore in a mullet style, which surprisingly suited him. He had a strong northern accent, deep and warm. There was no sexual chemistry between us; he was simply a good mate. I felt very comfortable in his company, safe even. We'd been friends for years and he was someone I knew I could always depend upon.

I took his arm and we walked down the road together. We were spoilt for cafés around here, and to be truthful, I really didn't care where we went, as long as it wasn't down Brook Street. We found a nice café with a quirky interior and ordered cappuccinos. I could talk to Jake about anything.

I met Jake years ago, through my brother Ash. Jake was a sometime roadie, and was full of great rock'n'roll stories, and scandals! I've often told him he should write a book about all of his experiences. He says he couldn't – people would either never believe the stories, or he'd get sued. Even though he made my life seem duller than I already believed it to be, I was entranced by his story telling.

I was very proud to have Jake as a friend, he was very cool, but also a 'ladies' man'. Maybe that was why I didn't fancy him, too much competition! He'd just returned from a metal tour up north and told me a funny story about the lead singer surfing the crowd and his trousers somehow got pulled down along the way (he wasn't wearing any boxers apparently) and he ended up surfing 'hanging loose' as it were, much to the delight of the girls I'm sure. Jake had to intervene to get him back on stage because the poor guy couldn't move his legs on account of his trousers being around his ankles! I'm guessing in that guy's eyes, Jake made hero status. There was another added bonus to having Jake as a friend, I sometimes got to go on a band's guest list.

We sat in the café for ages, passing the time talking and laughing about this and that. This was more like the carefree day I was expecting. My happiness had returned.

Chapter three

We were just sitting down at the table when I got a text from Charley. I read it in disbelief.

"No way!" I exclaimed.
"What?" Jake asked.
"You know the crash this morning I didn't tell you about?"
"Err, yeah?" replied Jake.
"Well, it seems like Charley's cousin's boyfriend was the guy in the car!"
Jake looked at me blankly.

"Charley just texted me, said she'd had a call from her mum asking her if she knew anything about a car crash on Brook Street this morning because she'd had her sister on the phone saying her daughter's boyfriend had been involved in a horrible car crash and was travelling up today to see him in hospital. Well, what are the chances?"
"Dun dun dun, six degrees of separation!" Jake replied.
"Oh Jake be serious, it's bad enough witnessing an accident without it involving someone you're connected with, albeit vaguely."
"Yep, that's the key word Dandie: vaguely. You don't even know Charley's cousin, let alone her boyfriend, do you?"
"Yeah, you're right Jake. It's just a bit weird."

Jake was, of course, right. I wish I could stop being reminded of this morning's crash though. It seemed that whatever distraction I created, something came back to haunt me. Maybe that's just typical of a state of shock, I didn't know. Maybe because it made such an impression I was almost seeking reminders of the event.

I wanted to move forward, really I did. I was so looking forward to a nice relaxing, uncomplicated day. It simply wasn't going to plan. I was starting to feel resentful, a bit like my nice day had been stolen from me.

Jake had to get back. I was on my own again. I thought about ringing Charley to get the latest on the bizarre connection, then thought better of it. She was probably busy writing her report. Anyway I was trying not to think about the morning's unfortunate events, I reminded myself.

So, a day off. What to do? I'd done meeting a friend, two even. Done shopping and coffee. I still had half a day left. It was bright and sunny, maybe a walk and a bit of much-needed exercise was called for.

I had nowhere in particular to walk to, so simply ambled along. I knew this town so well, every street corner, every alleyway. Most of them had some memory or other. I have never lived anywhere else. Always thought about moving to a different town, but somehow it never happened. I was still young, with plenty of time to move on if the situation arose, but frankly I was pretty happy here. I figured I was more of a dreamer than a doer.

For example, walking down the High Street, there's a night club above one of the major stores. The entrance is an inconspicuous heavy black door to the side of the building. In daylight it looks like nothing in particular, but come here after dark and you'll find a queue going around the corner and several huge bouncers on the door. I've had many a great night and adventures in there. Some I can remember more clearly than others, but on the whole they were memories of good times. I still go there on a night out when I can.

It used to be a venue for bands way back, and I'm told some really big names played there: The Stones, The Beatles and Jimi Hendrix to name just a few. Makes me smile that I have danced on the same floor as Mick Jagger! I don't think any major bands have played there since the late sixties however. We do get the occasional live band playing, but they're more local outfits, not big names. I suppose they've outgrown the venue.

It's a funny old place, once you entered the black door you're faced with a long narrow staircase. The club is above the shops so, up a couple of floors. The venue itself is poorly lit, and floor is sticky, I guess from numerous drink spillages. Once inside you could be anywhere really. There are no windows that I have ever noticed. At one end is a long, straight bar, at the other end a simple stage. In between a dance floor and some random seating. Oh, if walls could talk, there'd be some interesting tales for sure.

I like going there because they play rock music, which I love to dance to. Also, there are some really cool guys who go there too, major appeal. And of course, there are always friends and familiar faces, so it's a great place to catch up with people. All in all, an excellent night out.

It's not the only good club to go to of course, it's just the one that I go to most often. There are much better clubs for live music for instance. Distracted from my reminiscing of great nights out the phone rings; it's Charley, again.

"Hello Charley," I said.
"Dandelion, you'll never guess what!" Charley exclaimed.

13

"Surprise me," I replied.

"I've just received an email from Tom!"

"Tom? Tom, who?" I asked.

"The guy in Venice!"

I knew he'd get in touch with her, guys always did. Things like that would never happen to me, but they more often than not did happen to Charley. I was not surprised. I laughed.

"Well, what did he say?"

"I can't quite believe it, he says that he's coming my way today and would like to meet up. He's just got hold of some important information about Venice and the Lido he wants to show me!"

"Haha, how does he know where you live?"

"He doesn't, he just knows which town I live in. I didn't even know he had my email. It seems he's passing close by anyway and wanted to make a detour to meet up!"

"So are you meeting him?" I replied.

"Don't know, he sent the email last night – I've only just checked them as I was getting on with other stuff and didn't want to get into trawling through emails. He said, if it's ok, he'll ring me this morning."

"Has he rung?" I enquired.

"No," replied Charley, sadly. "Maybe he was waiting for me to reply. Damn!"

"So reply! Mind you, it might be a bit late, it's already half way through the day."

"I was thinking the same, but I'll reply anyway. Oh I hope I haven't missed him. I checked his email address and found out the company he works for, and his last name, result! He works in London, so I guess he lives there too? And his last name appears to be Bradley. Tom Bradley!"

"You'll make a detective yet." I laughed.

"Kind of goes with the territory Dandie."

"I guess, being a reporter. Well watch this space! Keep me posted won't you? On another note, what was this about the guy in the crash being your cousin's boyfriend?"

"Oh I know, how weird is that? Mum rang when I got home. It turns out that my cousin's boyfriend was involved in the crash this morning. She just rang me to see if I'd heard about it. When I told her it was outside your place, she couldn't believe it. I've never met him, and I don't see my cousin Beth that often, but my Mum and Aunt meet up regularly and so she hears all about Beth's life. Apparently he's a really nice guy, they've been together about three years, live together and everything. Anyhow, I'll maybe meet up with her later as she's coming to town."

"How far away does she live?" I asked Charley.

"She lives in London somewhere, North London I think. Not really sure because she moves quite often. Really Dandie, I only ever see her on family occasions. She's very nice, a few years younger than me. We used to see a lot of each other when we were younger, family holidays and get togethers, but since we've grown up and left home, I guess lives get busy and stuff. Anyhow, it would be cool to see her, if I can. I've texted her to say she's welcome to stay over at mine if she needed somewhere to stay while visiting hospital, that's if they keep him in of course, I don't know anything about his condition, do you?"

"No, all I know is that I saw the guy in the car staggering around looking confused, then the car blew up and it was pandemonium. What was he called?"

"Tom I think, not sure."

"Tom?" I repeated. "You don't think it could be the same Tom?"

"Same Tom as who?" Charley asked.

"Venetian Tom!" I suggested.

"No! No, don't be silly. Millions of people are called Tom," Charley replied.

"Suppose," I replied.

Charley paused on the phone, "I've really got to get on with some work, bye."

"Keep me posted," I replied.

I really hoped the car crash victim was ok. Now that there was, a somewhat tenuous, connection, I felt much better about thinking about the crash. Before it had somehow felt intrusive, as it was nothing to do with me I had no right to dwell on it. It had been someone else's tragedy which I had no right to gate crash. Now I felt that I had permission to find out more about the crash and those involved.

Chapter four

The town where I live is a typical, pretty, old English town. Medium sized I guess, not as big as Birmingham, but not as small as Norwich – just picking random places from the opposite sides of the country for comparison, could just as well be Manchester and Truro. Come to think of it Truro is probably closer in size. Anyhow, it's a well-established old town with some historical interest; I'm not quite up on all the intricate details, but I think there were some important battles nearby way back when people thought charging at one's opponent with nothing more than a long sword was a good idea. What a desperate thought, what must have gone through those guys' minds as they charged courageously into close combat?

Most of the buildings are very old, some even going back to Tudor times. There are modern buildings too of course, but they are mainly built on the outskirts of the town, as the centre is mostly protected under listed-building status. I love the character and history of all these old buildings. I often think what must life have been like, living here when they were built? Fascinating stuff, maybe I should have paid more attention to history lessons in school. Unfortunately while I was at school I had far more pressing things to worry about than history, things which now seem so trivial but at the time seemed so very important – you know: pop idols, parties, dates and the like.

Being a small town, nothing very extraordinary happens, I like that. I'm not too keen on surprises. Which brings me back unfortunately, to this morning's unwelcome surprise. As I had no particular plan to the rest of my day, I thought I would try to find out a little more about the crash.

I headed back home to see what, if anything, I could find out. I arrived to find the road still partially closed. The burnt out mangled mess of conjoined car and lorry was still there, although no longer smouldering. The blackened and crumpled car looked sinister and alien. Its seats had melted into a black solid mass. The lorry windscreen was smashed on the driver's side and the metal of the cab below was twisted and ragged with the front of the car somehow entwined within it. The car seemed to have suffered most from the blaze. The lorry having suffered fire damage mainly in the cab. It was a post-apocalyptic scene to be sure. The crowd had pretty much dispersed. There was a policeman standing 'guard' so I approached him and asked him how things were?

"All I know is that both drivers were taken to the hospital," he offered. Well that was a bit disappointing. Maybe the local paper would have more info. I went to the shop to buy it, but it wasn't on sale yet. I could check online, I really should get back to my flat anyway and make sure the smell had gone.

I had to ask permission from the policeman to return to my home. He kindly escorted me to the front door. I offered him a cup of tea as it seemed the polite thing to do, but he declined my offer. I climbed the stairs to my flat door and entered. The smell of burnt rubber was still pretty pungent. I opened all the windows to encourage some air circulation, put the kettle on and set up the laptop.

Sure enough there was an online story already about the crash, literally posted a few moments earlier. It didn't seem to say any more than I already knew, except...

I quickly picked up my phone and rang Charley.

"Hello," she said.

"Charley, they've given a name!" I exclaimed.

"A name?" Charley replied, slightly confused.

"The crash victims, they've named both drivers!"

"Oh?"

"Tom Bradley, from London!" I said.

Silence followed.

"Hello, Charley? Are you still there?" I asked, rather more urgently.

"It can't be..." Charley replied, clearly shocked.

"What are the chances?" I replied. This was a strange day indeed.

"So..." Charley started, hesitantly. "Tom, my cousin's boyfriend, is the same Tom that I met in Venice, and also the same Tom who crashed outside your flat this morning, possibly coming to town to visit me?"

"Maybe?"

"Now I need a brandy!"

Poor Charley. It seemed too fantastic a coincidence to be true, not to mention awkward. Did Beth know that Charley and Tom knew each other? Doubtful under the circumstances.

I finished on the phone with Charley, giving her time to take it all in. I wanted to start the whole day over again, this was way too complicated and stressful for a day off. I was even beginning to think that had I gone to work today, I would have missed the accident, known nothing about it, and not even questioned anything. It would have been just another day. That seemed a good option, unfortunately too late.

After a few minutes, Charley phoned back. She had spoken to her mother and told her all about 'Venice Tom'. Her mother had advised her to keep out of the way, that now was not the time for revelations. I agreed, and we both decided to watch further progressions from afar. Poor Charley, she felt responsible. I told her that he had been coming this way anyway, and to keep a perspective on events. We agreed to meet up later for more drinks.

I read a bit more of the article to see if there was any more information. All it said was that the name of the company the lorry driver worked for and that the car driver was on a business trip to meet up with a Sol Meadows of the environment agency.

Sol Meadows! *Sol Meadows, was my ex!* This was too weird, how many more coincidences could there be? Wow, Sol and I had been together for around four years. They were four very happy years as far as I was concerned. We even lived together for two of them. I can't believe that he too was linked to this morning's disaster. Jeez. I sat down on the sofa and stared vacantly into space. A random thought then crossed my mind, which never had before, amazingly. That was, had I married Sol, my name would have been Dandelion Meadows, how had I never thought of that before?
Then it occurred to me, *Sol may not know about the accident, why should he?* I felt duty bound to tell him.

I grabbed my phone. "Sol? Hi, It's Dandelion, how are you?"
"Hey Dandie, good, how about you?"
"Cool, Sol did you hear about the crash this morning?"
"Yes, I did, one of the guys was on his way to see me. Can you believe it? Why are you asking?" he asked, surprised.
"Yeah I can believe it Sol, there are so many connections with this Tom, it's freaky. Do you know him well?"

"Never met him," Sol replied. "He was coming up to talk to me about a project the company is working on. What are all these connections?"

I went on to explain to him all the strange linking threads.

"It feels a bit odd, that he was on his way to see me, bit surreal really. Not sure how I feel about that," Sol continued thoughtfully. "How are tricks with you Dandie, long time no see?"

"Same old, same old," I replied. My relationship with Sol was not altogether without its own complications.

As I said, we had four lovely years together. Then we broke each other's hearts. We were young and carefree, but we both had big dreams. He was very career driven, I was star struck. As time passed we drifted apart, he would become deadly serious about making his dream a reality – which, fair play – he succeeded in and is doing very well, thank you. Whereas I just carried on dreaming. Did I also mention that he resembled a Greek Adonis? We travelled the world together, we partied 'til dawn, we spent whole weekends in bed – we had fun. Then, he slept with another woman – a long story, and a lot of excuses later, I left him. As far as I was concerned that was the end of our relationship, I couldn't forgive him. He was then filled with remorse and self-pity and made several futile attempts to re-kindle our affair. Strangely I got over him fairly quickly; he'd broken my trust, and without trust, for me there was no going forward. I'm not saying it was easy, he'd hurt me badly, there were a lot of tears and heartache. It took him very much longer to get over me, and even now I think he would still entertain the idea of a reconciliation between us, but maybe that's just to relieve his guilt? Don't know and don't particularly care.

"Do you want to meet up? There's a gig next week at the town hall, great band, you'd love them. I could get tickets?" Sol offered.

"Sol, if he hadn't been coming to see you, Tom wouldn't have had the crash," I replied thoughtfully.

"The thought had crossed my mind, thanks for reminding me of that fact Dandie, I'd happily put it to the back of my head!"

"Sorry," I replied. I hadn't got the feeling that Sol had really taken on board the relevance of the connection, maybe I'd been wrong.

"Look Dandie, if you want to come to the gig, give me a shout, yeah. I've got to go."

That was Sol telling me to back off.

Chapter five

The doorbell rang, I went to the intercom. "Hello?"
"Dandie, it's Charley." I buzzed her in.
I stood at the top of the stairs waiting for Charley to appear.
"Hello, long time no see," I greeted her. For a working day, Charley didn't appear to be very productive.
"Oh don't, I couldn't focus on anything. Had to come and see you. Can't stop thinking about this morning and Tom. Do you know any more about the crash or any other news?"
"As it happens, yes. You'll never guess who Tom was coming up to meet?"

Charley looked at me blankly with an expectant expression. Charley had very dark, almost black thick hair. It was long, probably middle of her back in length. She wore it in a rockabilly style with Victory rolls. This matched her rockabilly dress sense, and Irregular Choice shoes, which she carried off well. She really did look as though she'd just walked out of a fifties B movie set.

"Well?" she asked, impatiently.
"Sol!"
"Your Sol?" Charley asked in disbelief.
"The very same – seriously what are the chances?"
"This is too weird!" Charley replied, astonished.
"Tell me about it!" I replied.
We both sat in silence for a few seconds, mulling over the convoluted events. As we sat there deep in thought, the doorbell rang again. I went to the intercom, it was the police. I let them in. There were two of them at my door, a man and woman. They entered into my flat and asked questions about the crash, how much I saw and what I had witnessed. It was pretty routine stuff, they had been to visit

anyone who lived nearby who may have seen what had happened, compiling witness statements.

I was beginning to wish I had stayed out. I know they have to gather as much information as possible, but at the same time, I didn't really want to keep reliving the experience. It was a chance for us to ask them questions though, but they weren't giving much away, and maybe they really didn't know anything. What I did establish was that both casualties were doing ok, they were both in hospital still, but neither injuries were life threatening. That was a huge relief. Neither Charley nor I let on about any of the weird connections we had with Tom, it didn't seem appropriate, trivial even, given the circumstances.

"What actually happened?" I asked them, I had only heard the crash and seen the aftermath.
"According to eye witnesses, the lorry was going quite fast, but the car was on the wrong side of the road, or had taken the bend too sharply, or simply lost control of the wheel, and the two vehicles collided." The policeman responded in a matter of fact way. They took a note of my personal details and left.

"Well, this has turned out to be a fun day," I said casually to Charley.
"Sure has," she replied thoughtfully. "You know my cousin Beth is one lucky lady to have Tom as her boyfriend."
"Hmm," I replied. "She must be in town by now, it doesn't take that long to get here from London."
"At least you don't have to feel guilty about him coming here to visit you, we know now that he was coming to see Sol."

"Yeah, how strange is that! I like Sol, you two were a good couple you know."

"Don't even go there," I replied. My relationship with Sol was history, that was that.

My phone rang, it was Ash, my brother. Ash only ever rang if he was in trouble, or wanted something.

"Hi Ash, what you after?"

"An audience with my gorgeous sister, if that's ok."

"OK, Ash, spill."

"I received a letter the other day, a really odd one. I didn't tell you, because, to be honest, I thought it was a prank."

"Go on, you have my attention," I replied.

"Well. As I was saying, I got this letter, from a guy who wanted to meet up with me, said he had a family connection with us..."

"Us?" I repeated.

"Yeah, I didn't tell you, because I thought it was a wind up. Anyhow, I'm meeting him at 1pm, wondered if you wanted to come along?"

"Ash, why are you asking me now, and why are you going to meet a total random stranger?"

"Curiosity darling, that's all. I wasn't going to go, that's why I didn't tell you. But I thought 'what the hell', it could be nothing, but it could be something interesting. Anyhow, as he mentioned you too, thought I'd give you a shout."

"Thanks for the notice Ash! How long have you known about this meeting?"

"About a week," he replied, unfazed.

I thought about it, 1pm was in half an hour. It wasn't a lot of time, but I needed to get out of the flat anyway and had no other plans.

Ash was a couple of years older than me. He was a lot of fun, we got on really well and had always been close. He only lived on the other side of town. We had a younger sister too, Rose, but neither of us were that close to her. She was very independent and frankly, self-obsessed. If it didn't revolve around her it wasn't important. She was quite hard work, as a result neither Ash nor I saw that much of her if we could help it.

"He mentioned me?" I said, thoughtfully. "Why not, ok. Do you have any more details: who is he, why does he want to meet up, what family connection?"
"I'll pick you up in the car and tell you everything I know then – which isn't much really, thanks for coming mate."
"Yeah, whatever," I replied. This was typical of Ash, everything was last minute with him.

I told Charley about Ash's call, and we both got ready to leave the flat.

"Ash can drop you off at home," I said to Charley.
"That's ok, I'll walk, and it's not far. Let me know how the mystery meeting goes, won't you. I could do with something else to think about today."
"Sure thing, it'll be nothing though. Probably just one of Ash's friends playing a joke on him. It'll be good to see Ash though." With that Charley and I parted our ways, she headed back to her place while I waited on the doorstep for Ash. I should have told him about the crash and the road being closed. Too late now, he'd be on his way. He'll find out soon enough.

Sure enough, after waiting for about five minutes, I got a call from Ash.
"Dandie, your road's blocked, I'm around the corner in the Strand, see you in a sec."

26

I walked past the wreckage. They were beginning to clear things up a bit. It was a big mess, horrible to see the vehicles so crumpled and burnt, it must have been terrifying for the drivers. There were still people in fluorescent jackets and hard hats, making notes and writing things down. Traffic was slowly moving on the other side of the road, single file. Police were directing the traffic.

I saw Ash's car parked haphazardly half on the pavement. "Hello," I said as I got into the car. "What's going on in your road?" Ash asked. I filled him in on all the mornings' drama. "So, what do we know about this guy and where are we meeting him?" I asked. "Don't know much, the letter was all a bit cryptic really. He said that he'd found a family connection with us, he was researching his family tree or something, and would it be ok to meet."

I was intrigued. If it was genuine, this could be interesting, I know pretty much all there is to know about our family, but haven't done a family tree. So if someone else had researched our family, it could be interesting. It was certainly a relief to have something else to think about today.

Ash had arranged to meet in a central tourist spot, a café that overlooked a large pedestrianised square with some sort of memorial at the centre. We parked the car and made our way to the café. "How are we going to know who he is?" I asked. "I hadn't thought of that," Ash replied. "Although, he did give me his number, we could phone him?" It was almost 1pm, we both bought drinks and found a window seat.

"How are you anyway?" Ash asked. "You must have been pretty shaken up by the crash. Very rude of them to have an accident right outside your place I say."

"I'm ok, tell you what though, there have been some really odd connections with one of the casualties."

Chapter six

Ash and I waited for about an hour, the time passed quickly, we talked about this and that. He was a very talented musician and played guitar in a moderately successful Indie rock band. He spent much of his time touring playing gigs, and they'd had some chart success too. He always made me laugh with his stories of life on the road. He had fun, but he also worked hard. Being a 'rock star' is not as glam as you might think.

While we were chatting and laughing, we'd almost forgotten the reason we were there, to meet the 'mystery' man.

"Ash, we've been here ages, he hasn't shown. I reckon it's one of your mates winding you up," I said suddenly aware of how much time had passed.

"Yeah, think you're right, best get moving. When I find out who set this up…"

"How about you ring him?" I suggested, seemed obvious really. We'd been so preoccupied chatting we'd forgotten that Ash had his number. At least then we'd find out who the prankster was.

"Good thinking sis!" Ash replied, and searched for the number and dialled.

The phone rang for several rings, then answered.

"Hello?" a female said, nervously.

"Who is this?" Ash said, realising that this must be a set up.

"Umm, this is Tom's phone, who is this?"

"Tom who?" Ash replied.

"Umm, Tom Bradley," the woman replied hesitantly. "Who are you? Tom's been in an accident, this is his girlfriend. He's unconscious."

Ash was silenced for a few seconds – very unusual for him, he then composed himself and explained about the meeting and how he'd thought it may be a hoax. The girl on the end of the phone said Tom had a few meetings planned – they were now cancelled, and that was the end of that. She hung up.

Ash relayed the conversation back to me. I was dumbstruck, surely it couldn't be the same Tom Bradley, seriously, *who was this guy?* And what on earth was his connection with me and my family? This was getting altogether way too crazy and close for comfort.

"This is just silly," was pretty much all Ash could think of to say. I went over with him all the bizarre connections there had been with this Tom Bradley throughout the morning. Then together, we tried to imagine what on earth his connections could be with our family. As I said before I had a pretty good knowledge of our family history, it wasn't very extraordinary. Our mother and father have been happily married for ever, they had three children, and we have one aunt, two uncles and five cousins. Both sets of grandparents were still around, though frail and a little confused sometimes. But we were an ordinary family. Ash and I really couldn't see where this guy could possibly fit in.

"I could ask Rose if she knows anything?" Ash suggested.
"OK," I replied. I didn't think she would know anything that we didn't know, but it was worth a try.
Ash rang her phone but there was no answer. "I'm probably not important enough to talk to," he said sarcastically. I laughed. I had to admit, I was becoming quite obsessed

with Tom Bradley, and was keen to know what his connection might be with our family.

"You could ask Mum?" I suggested.
"OK," Ash said. He rang her. Our mother, Sylvia, is a gentle, kind, and loving person. She always has time for everyone. She is quite quiet, our dad is the big talker of the family, but she is always there when you need her. Nothing is ever too much trouble.

She and our father had got together quite young and had all three of us in their early twenties, so they were comparatively young parents. They had lived a pretty alternative life in their twenties, living in squats in London, going on peace rallies and generally protesting for the good in humanity to overthrow the consumer-thirsty, money-greedy capitalistic society which they saw developing quickly around them. They named their children after flowers or trees.

They mellowed as they got older, got good jobs, moved out of London, bought a house in an altogether more relaxed and rural town, swapping their protest banners for organic vegetable plots and homemade wine. Dad is a graphic designer, he started off his career designing record sleeves and then he was headhunted for a big design company. He liked his work and was able to work mainly from home. Mum had spent most of her life bringing us up and blossomed late in life as a counsellor.

"Hello darling, how are you?" she answered, pleased to hear from Ash.
Ash explained about the strange communication he had with Tom.

Mum seemed nonplussed. "It's probably just a mix up, surely?" she replied.

Ash told her as much as he knew, not much admittedly, but he told her that Tom believed he had a family connection with us. She didn't recognise his name.

The phone went quiet. "Mum, are you there, hello?" Ash said, "I think she's gone," he said to me, perplexed.

"I'm still here," she replied.

"Are you ok, you sound...different?" Ash asked concerned.

"Did he say what his connection was?"

"No, I think he'd been investigating his family tree, or something, and found that we were part of it? He's probably just got mixed up with some other family," Ash offered.

"How old is he?" Sylvia asked.

"No idea," Ash replied.

"Where is he?" She asked.

"In hospital, he was involved in a car crash this morning, outside Dandie's place. Why are you so interested?" Ash didn't like the way the conversation was going.

"Oh no, poor guy. How awful, does he have anyone with him?" Mum seemed a little too interested in this guy. Was there something she knew that she hadn't told us?

"Mum, you're making me nervous, why all the questions, you don't know him do you?"

The phone had gone quiet again.

"Mum?" Ash said. She'd hung up.

"What the hell?" Ash said, looking blankly at the phone in disbelief. "She hung up on me, what the ...?"

"She's never done that before," I said. "How very strange, how did she sound?" I asked.

"Weird! She sounded weird Dandie. Not like Mum at all. She sounded shocked and a little too interested for my liking."

"Maybe it was because he was involved in an accident?" I offered.

"Umm, I don't think so. Why was she asking so many questions about him?" Ash said, almost to himself.

"She was trying to work out who he was?" I replied, trying to help. "Could she tell you anything?" I asked.

"No, but I think she knew something." Ash replied. "Why did she hang up?" he repeated.

"I don't know, it could be for any number of reasons. Maybe she didn't. Maybe her phone battery went flat?" I offered.

"Yeah, you're probably right Dandie, she's not exactly a techy is she?"

Chapter seven

Our early childhood years had been pretty chaotic, but in a fun way. As I said, our parents were quite radical lefties, always going on marches and demos supporting human rights and environmental issues mainly. We lived in various squats in London. I have very fond memories of one in particular in west London which we must have lived in for several years. It was actually three terraced houses, all squatted by various people and families. The houses seemed huge to me as a child, three stories each, with huge spaces inside them. We used to ride our bicycles up and down the hallways. Although each house had a front door, it was possible to go between the houses without actually leaving the buildings. I think some holes in the walls had been created between each house, so it was in effect, one big communal building.

The garden was the best thing though. The old brick walls between each of the three, large by London standards, gardens had all but collapsed, creating a large open space for us kids to play in. It was like an adventure playground. The adults had built various structures for us, a tree house, climbing frame, swings, tunnels and more. There were always other children to play with, and we were pretty much left to our own devices, but an adult was never far away if we needed a sandwich or a plaster.

It was a very sociable existence, people were always coming and going, meal times were chaotic, busy and fun. There were always lots of people at the dinner table and we had to pretty much fight over food; there was no hanging around or polite waiting to be served, we had to grab what we could as there was a lot of competition. It was similar with bathing. We didn't have a bath very often, maybe once a week, and there were always several children in the bath at the same time. Some squats didn't have hot water, so it made sense for us all to get in the bath together after all the kettle boiling that was involved in filling up the tub. It was the way we lived and it was fun.

The transient people didn't really register to me as a child, it was all part of normal life. There was a very good underground communication system around London at the time. People would earmark potential squats and organise the opening of them. There were rules about opening squats, ideally without involving 'criminal damage', so the opening was usually done a couple of days ahead of a family moving in. Some squats were better suited to families, others to single people, but mostly it was a peaceful, respectful acquisition of property which was lying vacant, usually due for demolition. It was unusual to stay in a squat for more than a year, so apart from the one I've already told you about, we moved often.

The constant moving, however, was stressful, especially for my mother. She was trying to create a stable environment for our family, but the insecurity of knowing we may have to move at short notice was in conflict to her ideal.

When Rose started school, my parents decided to leave London and settle in a quieter town. Squatting was becoming more difficult and was attracting some aggressive hangers on, so my parents felt they no longer wanted to be part of it all. Their ideal had been to make good use of perfectly habitable housing for as long as possible, on peaceful and compliant terms. A new breed of squatters had jumped on board, whose objectives were more militant and destructive. My parents felt the time had come to

35

distance themselves and our family from the London scene. We moved into a rented house in this pretty town. The house seemed tiny to me, but it wasn't the house that was small, it was the size of the rooms. It felt cramped.

I hated the move at first. I was used to having children to play with and people around me all the time. There had always been something happening. Suddenly life had become very quiet. The house was still, even with five of us living together. I missed the constant noise and comings and goings of our previous life style.

Anyhow, children are very adaptable, and we were a close family, we had each other. We soon settled into our new lifestyle. We made a few mistakes, of course. Going from squatting in London to living a relatively conventional existence in a rural town was never going to be a smooth transition. As an adult I can perfectly understand and sympathise with our change of circumstances, but as a seven-year-old child, I was cross and resentful.

Those early childhood years seem a lifetime ago now. I admire our parents for their strength of belief and character, but also, I'm very glad we did move out of London. It gave us all stability and a sense of security and permanence, belonging even, that we didn't have until then.

You see them now, with their nice house, car, good jobs, and it's hard to imagine that not so long ago they were living this radical alternative lifestyle. It makes me laugh really thinking about it. They still hold the same beliefs and opinions, their protests are much quieter these days, but no doubt still as strong and effective.

Dad was lucky, he is a very talented artist, and had made lots of connections within the music world while living in London. Many, now very well-known and successful bands were squatting too and they were our friends. People loved his artwork and he was soon in high demand for album cover artwork. He was always working on one album sleeve or another. This gave him the financial opportunity to move away, eventually buying a house, and still support the family. He now works on more commercial and varied graphic design projects. He is always busy, and mostly enjoys his work. I think it can be pressured at times, but he pretty much takes things in his stride.

Ash's phone rang, it was Mum.

"Ash, what do you know about Tom Bradley's condition?"

"Nothing," Ash replied, confused by the question.

"Oh," Mum replied, disappointed.

"Mum, what's going on, do you know something about this guy?"

"Maybe," she replied.

"Well, spill," Ash replied, becoming irritated with her vagueness.

"Well…" she replied hesitantly, "I think I may know who he is, but I need to see him first."

Ash interrupted her conversation to relay to me what she was saying. I took the phone from him.

"Mum, what do you know about this guy?" I asked directly.

"Do you know how he is?" she asked, ignoring my question.

"No, all I know is that he was in a car crash this morning and he's now in hospital."

"Ok, don't worry, I'm sure everything will become clear," she replied.

"Everything will become clear – what are you on about? If there's something we should know…"

"Haha, nothing for you to worry about darling. Why don't you come to dinner this weekend?" she asked. It was her way of diverting the conversation away, and I knew it.

"Yeah, ok, see you then," I replied and ended the conversation.

"What's she hiding?" I asked Ash.

"Something!" he replied.

We mulled over all the possibilities of connections Tom Bradley could have with our family, the only tangible thing we could come up with was that he must have lived in the same squat as us at some point, many people did. We would have to wait until the weekend to find out more.

Chapter eight

"So, what are you up to for the rest of the day?" I asked Ash.

"Well, not sure really. I'd pretty much written it of on account of meeting this curious guy. Don't know what to think about it really."

"Nothing," I replied. "There's nothing to think about. My day has been completely hijacked by this morning's events. I for one am more than ready to move on."

Ash laughed and gave me a hug.

"C'mon, Dandie, loosen up. Let's get out of here."

With that we grabbed our things and left the café. The sun was still shining, it was a glorious afternoon.

When I wasn't having spectacular dramas unfolding literally on my door step, my life was really rather ordinary. I worked for a local company, mainly doing admin. It was ok, not the dream career I'd anticipated for myself. I was effectively happily plodding along, waiting for my dream career/life to present itself. I'm single, it's ok, I would like a man in my life, but I'm not desperate. There were definite positives to being a young single lady. There were probably more to being in a happy relationship, but I wasn't going to dwell on those. Basically I'm quite happy with my lot. I'm still young and have my whole life ahead of me. Hey anything could happen in the next twelve months. I could meet a rich prince, I could be swept off my feet onto a jet plane to the Seychelles, I could win the lottery and become a millionaire. My fairy-tale dream life could become a reality – couldn't it? No, I didn't think so either.

Ash and I walked through town. I love Ash to bits, we get on so well, we are like soul mates really. He is one of the few people who really understands me, and likewise I really understand him. Rose is very different to us. She is serious about everything. Fair play to her she's doing very well for herself. She has a great job as a PA to some bigwig, never really understood what it is he does. Anyhow, she's at his beck and call. I really think he'd be lost without her. She drives a nice car, has a very nice (but ordinary) flat which she owns – can you believe it! She has a fiancé called David. He's quite a bit older than her, ten years I think. David's ok, can't say I know him well. Even though they've been together for years, we rarely see either of them. I get the impression that our family are a bit beneath David and Rose. Their social life is really quite highbrow. I think we're the embarrassing in laws, to be hidden out of sight. It upsets Mum a lot. She loves Rose as much as the rest of us, but she is an enigma for sure.

Just as we were walking along the pavement, me linking arms with Ash, we noticed that we were being followed by a small group of teenage girls.
"Haha, it's the fan club," I whispered to Ash.
He stopped and turned to the girls. There were three of them. When Ash stopped, they all stopped too. Looking awkward, they started to giggle, then one of the girls came up to us.
"Can I have a photo taken with you?" she asked him, completely ignoring my presence, I was for all intents and purposes, invisible.
"Sure", he responded, lapping up the adulation.
She flung herself at him and took a photo on her mobile phone. She then cheekily pecked him on the cheek, went back to her friends and the three of them turned to each other and huddled around the phone to look at the photo. Ash and I continued walking.

"Haha, that was hilarious, you sly dog you!" I laughed teasingly at Ash.

"Can't help being irresistible can I?" he jokingly replied.

This sort of thing happened more often than you would imagine. It still shocks me a little, and makes me smile. Ash is my brother, I forget that to many he is a moderately famous rock star, an idol even to some. He does take advantage of his 'rock star' status sometimes, who can blame him really? He doesn't have a girlfriend at the moment, but has more than his fair share of female admirers and consequently, flings. He has a laissez-faire attitude to sex, which I do rib him about. But he's having a good time, I'd probably do the same in his shoes. I'm may be just a little jealous of the attention he receives in reality.

Ash is tall and willowy. He has ginger hair, which he regularly dyes different colours and messes about with. No matter what colour his hair is though, he cannot change his pale and freckly English complexion. He is not what you would call 'good looking', but he does have enormous charisma, and is quite quirky looking. He is big on personality, always very friendly and warm to people, he's like Dad in that way. Pretty outgoing, he does get up to mischief, but never gets into any serious trouble. He generally enjoys life and makes the best of any given situation. He always has a positive slant on things. Ash is the polar opposite of Rose. I guess I sit somewhere in the middle, I think I'm more like mum really.

"You know Dandie, you have your fair share of admirers too," Ash said.

"Yeah, sure!" I replied.

"Seriously, guys are always coming up to me and asking about you."

"No they're not Ash, you tease."

"Seriously Dandie, you just don't pick up on the subtle hints do you?"

"Because there are none," I replied, not believing a word Ash was saying. I'm sure I'd know if someone was remotely interested in me.

"There you go," Ash said.

"There I go what?" I replied.

"Those two guys who just walked past us, they both turned to look at you. You turn heads Dandie, you just don't see it."

"Nonsense, Ash. I'm walking down the street with a semi-legendary rock star, really who do you think they're looking at?"

"Oh, Dandie, you just let life pass you by. You need to grab the opportunities as they present themselves. Nothing's going to happen unless you make it."

"Yeah, whatever," I replied, things never did happen to me, end of.

Ash's words didn't fall completely on deaf ears, even if I didn't believe them, it made me smile to hear some flattery.

"It's a nice day Ash, how about we take a boat out?" The day had not been the best, I was desperate for a change of scene and a distraction from all that had transpired today. We have a pretty river running through and alongside the town, it is possible to hire row boats for an hour or so. It wasn't something I did often, but it seemed a good idea right now. Ash agreed and we made our way along to the boating station.

Chapter nine

It was mid-afternoon when we arrived, and being a lovely day we were not the only people with rowing boats on their mind. We waited for about fifteen minutes for a boat to become available. The boathouse was an interesting black and white Victorian building with a large shed attached, I guess that's where the boats were stored. There was a sloping decked area leading to the water's edge where the boats pulled in.

After a pleasant but long wait, a rather attractive boat-master helped me and Ash onto our row boat. I sat back and relaxed and Ash sat in the middle of the boat with the oars.
"I see how it is," he said.
I looked at him blankly.
"You assumed I'd do the rowing didn't you?"
"Yes," I replied, in a coy manner.
"Hmm, well little sis', I'll make a deal. I'll row out and you can row back, ok?"
"Ok," I replied, with no intention at all of honouring our agreement.

Ahh this is the life, I thought to myself as we made our getaway from the hustle and bustle downriver into a world of water lilies and willow trees with their long, delicate branches overhanging the river bank. It was quiet and still, apart from the odd passing boat, and people sitting on the riverbank with their fishing rods and flasks.

"We should have brought a picnic," I suggested.
"At the very least a bottle of wine," replied Ash.
"We didn't come prepared did we?" I said.

"Not very well planned Dandie," agreed Ash.

I rested back on the wooden slatted seat and trailed my hand in the water, finally I felt relaxed, and for the first time that day I actually felt as though I was having the kind of day off I had expected. I could have closed my eyes and fallen asleep. I loved the stillness of the river. My eyes began to glaze over as I watched the ripples in the water, when something caught my attention.

"What's that over there Ash?" I asked. I could see an animal swimming along the edge of the river.
"Probably a water rat," he suggested.
I peered closer. "I think it's an otter, row towards it Ash."
"It's never going to be an otter!" Ash exclaimed, but did turn course slightly and headed towards the riverbank.
We became entangled in the draping branches of an overhanging willow.
"Ash, you've crashed!"
The boat had lost its course and the end had banked.
"Great, we're stuck now."
"No we're not Dandie, just pull on the branches to get us out of here," Ash instructed.
We had become well and truly entangled in a mass of overhanging willow branches.
"We could push ourselves off with an oar," I suggested, and took one of the oars and started to push into the mud bank with it. As I did this I spotted some paper floating in the water. I caught it with the oar and brought it onto the boat for closer inspection. It wasn't paper, it was a fifty pound note!
"Ash!" I exclaimed, then I looked closer at the riverbank. I could just make out a small plastic bag. "Ash, get us closer to the bank."
"Closer?" he replied confused, but obliged.

As we got closer I stretched the oar out as far as I could to try and get to the bag, but couldn't quite reach it.

"Ash, we need to get right up close."

"What do you see Dandie?" he asked.

"I'm not sure… I think…"

We were very close now, I stretched over as far as I could. The bag was wedged into the mud of the river bank. I just managed to grab a tiny piece of the plastic, but it wasn't enough to pull it out.

"Hold onto me Ash, I'm going to grab that bag."

"Ok?"

I grabbed hold of a branch and tried to pull us closer, but the boat wouldn't budge.

"Dandie, what are you doing?" Ash asked.

"I need to get to that bag," I replied.

"It's a dirty plastic bag!" he said.

"I think it may have something in it." Ash hadn't noticed the fifty pound note I had found, and in my excitement I'd forgotten to tell him.

With Ash holding onto my waist I managed to lean right out of the boat and with one hand on the muddy river bank I managed to grab the bag with my other hand. Ash pulled me back into the boat.

I put the bag on the floor. It was old and the plastic had become discoloured and brittle. I opened it up, it wasn't sealed, inside was the biggest wodge of money I had ever seen. A stack of fifty pound notes, no less!

"Blimey!" Ash cried out.

I looked up at Ash speechless.

"What the hell?" I said.

"What do we do now?" I asked.

"Count," suggested Ash.

We counted the money, twenty-eight in all. Twenty-eight fifty pound notes!

Ash and I looked at each other shocked.

"£1400!" I whispered to him.

"Drug money," he stated.

"Oh no!" I replied, suddenly scared.

"Don't worry," said Ash, "It's obviously been lying around for very long time, it's probably been lost or something."

I suddenly felt uneasy, I'd watched far too many gangster movies, all sorts of paranoid thoughts suddenly raced through my brain.

"Or it could simply be dropped tourist money," Ash offered some attempt at reassurance.

"Ash, no tourist carries that amount of cash around with them." I exclaimed.

"You'd be surprised."

I felt much more reassured thinking it was misplaced tourist money rather than drug money.

"So, what do we do with it?" I asked.

"Umm, keep it," Ash replied, as though it was a foregone conclusion.

"Don't you think someone may be missing it?" I asked.

"I think someone most definitely is missing it," he replied, "but, let's face it, they've been missing it for a very long time. How long do you think that bag's been there for?"

"Fair point," I replied. I felt in a dilemma, I mean, if I'd lost that amount of money, it'd be such a big deal. It could be someone's life savings, anything. Should we take it to the police? Then I thought about the time issue. I don't know the exact life span of a plastic bag, but I'm pretty sure it takes more than a few weeks to look like this one.

I Googled *'What to do with lost and found money'* on my phone.

"Ash, the law says you have to hand it in to the police, if it is not claimed in 28 days, you get to keep it."

"Well, think about it Dandie, this money has been lying around for a lot longer than twenty eight days, I say we keep it."

The more I thought about, the more I agreed. It had been there for a long time. It's a strange place to lose that amount of money, I mean if it had been dropped in the street, it would be a different matter.

I could certainly do with the money. Yep, my mind was made up, keep it.

"Yay! Ash, we get to keep all this money, wow!" I said excitedly. "Half each?" I suggested.

"Nah, you found it, you keep the grand and I'll take the £400."

"No way, Ash, split 50/50."

"Shut up Dandie, I'm not arguing. Take it, you need it more than me anyway."

Well, either way, this find had certainly brightened up my day's outlook. I'd sort out the financial distribution later.

I now had a fixed smile on my face, as we negotiated getting off the mud bank and out of the willow canopy back into the flow of the river.

"Now we really could do with a bottle to celebrate!" I giggled.

Ash laughed and rowed heroically along the river. I held the plastic bag tightly on my lap, as though it were a small creature that would wriggle free at the slightest chance.

"What the hell was I going to do with all this money?" I thought happily to myself.

Chapter ten

Distracted by our fortuitous find, the boat trip rather lost its appeal. We rowed back to the boating station, (I have to say that Ash did row all the way, I knew he would). We were met by the same gorgeous looking boatman who'd set us up with the boat. I caught his eye and smiled. I don't know if it was the euphoria of the money find which gave me the confidence to make eye contact and smile, or if it was his engaging persona. Whichever, to my surprise my smile was reciprocated. I left the boating station with a skip in my step and an even bigger grin on my face. I gave a casual glance back over my shoulder as Ash and I made our way out of the boathouse and as I did the boatman looked up at me and smiled again while attending to the boat. *Score!* I thought happily to myself.

As we walked along the road back into town and away from the riverside, me holding tightly onto the old plastic bag, we passed a local newspaper seller. There on the front page was a large photo of this morning's car crash, and below it were two photos, one of each of the drivers involved. I bought a copy. Ash and I stopped by a low wall, which we sat upon and together looked at the front page. The crash photo seemed a little too intense and graphic for my liking. I was more interested in seeing a picture of Tom Bradley. There was nothing extraordinary about him. He had a pleasant face, short dark hair, clean shaven. I read the write up to see if there was any more information. Disappointingly there was nothing which I didn't already know. He was traveling up from London on a business trip when he collided with the lorry in Brook Street. It did suggest that he may have been distracted by his mobile phone. Was that what had caused him to be on the wrong side of the road? The newspaper article implied that he was unconscious and still in hospital.

Ash was interested in the photo of Tom Bradley.
"You know, he looks vaguely familiar, I can't quite place him though," Ash said, staring closely at the photograph.
"Really? You think you may know him?" I asked, surprised.
"I don't know, there's just something about him."
"Hmm, I think too much thought has been given to this guy, we're beginning to imagine things now. He looks like lots of people," I replied. Ash agreed and no more was said on the matter.

I carefully wrapped the plastic bag containing the money in the newspaper, in an attempt to disguise it and we headed back to my flat where we would share the cash out. Hopefully now the road would be cleared and everything would have returned to normal.

It was now late afternoon, but it was still a lovely sunny day. Ash and I were quiet making our way back home. I was in a thoughtful mood. Smiling to myself about the money find and the boatman. What a strange day it had been. I began to think about the money and what I could do with it. It was a lot of money, but it wasn't a life changing amount. I could pay off some debts, buy some new clothes, a bicycle or just put it in the bank for a rainy day...or I could just blow it and have a fantastic night out! Ash was all for blowing the money in one go. Ash could party, he had boundless amounts of energy and stamina and I always joked that he had taken mine and Rose's my share.

We arrived at my flat, the road outside was still closed in one lane but it had finally been cleared and things were beginning to return to normal. I paused in thought for a second outside the front door. Looking around me I thought, *had I gone to work as normal today, I would have left before the crash and returned after the road had been cleared, and quite possibly would never have known there had been an incident.* Which made me think, *how funny it is that the slightest change in plan could affect so much.* Food for thought indeed.

We made our way upstairs. I put the bag on the table and put the kettle on. Ash opened up the bag and laid all the money out on the table top.

"Wow," he said, "I've never seen so much cash!"

I went over to look at it, and burst out laughing. "Yay!" was all I could think of to say. "We must take a photo," I said and took a picture on my phone.

Ash and I sat with our cups of tea discussing what each of us would do with our share.

"I'm going to spend it on a night out!" exclaimed Ash. No surprises there, I thought.

"We could go traveling," I suggested.

"Could do," Ash replied thoughtfully. "Where would we go?" he continued.

"Venice!" I exclaimed excitedly, without hesitation.

I was so excited about the thought of going to Venice, I really couldn't think of anywhere else I'd like to go. I began looking at places to stay, checking the weather report. When was the best time to go? I would have to book time off work. How long should I go for? I wanted to talk it all over with Charley, after all she had just returned from the wonderful city, and had been there several times. She would know all the best places to go and would have lots of good advice.

I was having fun planning, but I don't think Ash was that inspired really. The thing is that with his band he already travels quite a bit, so it's not as exciting to him as it is to someone like me who never goes anywhere.

"We could book it right now Ash, just like that," I suggested.
Ash laughed, "Go on then why not?"
We got online and started looking at flights. I was so excited.

My phone rang, bizarrely it was Charley.
"Hello Charley, I was just thinking about you!" I said, excitedly. "You'll never guess what Ash and I just found," I excitedly told Charley about the money and my travel plans, she was suitably impressed.
"On another matter," Charley said in a much more serious tone, "I have my cousin Beth here with me, she would like to meet you."
"Really, why?" I replied, surprised.
"I can't tell you on the phone, is it ok if we come over now?
"Yep, sure," I replied.
"Strange," I said to Ash. "Charley's cousin wants to meet me, why would she want to meet me?"
"Because you're Charley's friend," Ash replied as though it were obvious.
"Hmm…" I wasn't convinced, surely under the circumstances she would have much more important things on her mind like the welfare of her boyfriend. But I gave her the benefit of doubt, maybe she just needed a change of scene, or maybe she wanted to see what I knew about the crash. It was a shame though, because I was very happy planning my trip to Venice and wasn't really in the mood for making new acquaintances, especially ones with emotional baggage right now.

The doorbell rang shortly afterwards, it was Charley. We put the money away and my travel plans on hold and I let her in.

"Hello," she said as she got to the flat door. "This is my cousin Beth."

With Charley was a petite young woman with shoulder length fair hair.

"Hi, I'm Beth, Charley's cousin, you must be Dandie?" she reached out her hand to me. She seemed friendly enough.

I shook her hand and invited them both in.

"This is Ash, my brother," I explained to Beth. She approached him and told him how pleased she was to meet him.

It all seemed a little bit odd and overly familiar to me. Here I was minding my own business, planning a fabulous trip, and happily dreaming about gorgeous boatmen, being rudely brought back down to earth with the introduction of someone I had no interest whatsoever in meeting. I was a bit miffed to be honest, and I hoped they wouldn't stay long so I could get on with my exciting plans.

"I'm so glad you're both here," Beth continued. I looked at Charley, confused. She looked back at me with an expression of sadness, which made me even more confused.

Ash and I sat down and waited to see what Beth would say next.

"I think you both know why I'm here?" she said, tentatively.

"Umm, no, not really," I replied, "I mean, I know that you've come to town to see your boyfriend who was involved in a crash. How is he by the way?"

"He's still unconscious I'm afraid, so we don't really know much." She paused. "I understand that Tom arranged to meet up with you, Ash?" she said looking at Ash.

"Well, I think so. I'm a bit confused about it all really," he replied, and continued, "Maybe you could put us in the picture?"

Beth took a deep breath. She looked tired and stressed, not surprisingly really. I don't think I'd look too great if I found out my boyfriend had been in a crash, driven for two hours and found him unconscious.

"Hmm, don't quite know how to put this..." Beth continued. "Tom had been doing some digging around into his past. He has always known that he was adopted. He had lovely parents and a loving upbringing. His mother recently died; it's a long story, and he felt that he wanted some answers about his background."

Ash and I looked at each other, confused. *What on earth could this have to do with us?*

"It would seem..." Beth hesitated and looked to Charley for reassurance. Charley nodded. "...that your mother, Sylvia Fisher, is Tom's birth mother."

Stunned silence followed, Ash and I looked at each other in utter disbelief. Then Ash exploded.

"What!" Ash exclaimed. "What on earth are you talking about?" he seemed angry.

"I'm sorry, you must be mistaken. Charley, I think you should both leave!" I said quickly.

"But Dandie..." Charley pleaded.

"Please go." I said calmly but firmly.

Beth looked awkward and sad; they both picked up their bags and reluctantly left.

Chapter eleven

"What the hell!" Ash shouted, he was really cross. "How dare some random stranger come into your flat and tell us fantasy stories about our mother! How dare she!"

Ash was pacing around the flat, his face all tense and furrowed.

"What was Charley thinking of? Idiot. Seriously Dandie, she is well out of order mate!"

"Calm down Ash," was all I could think of saying. I was stunned and confused by their visit and disappointed in Charley for bringing Beth around to see us. It was very badly handled, she should never have come.

"You know what that silly girl said is pure fabrication don't you, Dandie?" Ash said firmly to me.

"Yes," I replied hesitantly. "Well, I think so. We'd know if mum had another child, wouldn't we?"

"How dare she come around and say such things, how dare she!" Ash continued ranting and pacing, completely ignoring me.

"Ash, go home. Go and get some fresh air and forget all about this. The girl's obviously got us mixed up with someone else. Forget it," I suggested. I needed him to go, he was completely over reacting.

"You're right, sorry. I'm just amazed that anyone could just turn up and say something like that. She must be crazy!" Ash kissed me abruptly on the cheek and left, slamming the door behind him.

As soon as he'd gone I realised he'd left his share of the money behind. I shouted after him, but he'd run down the stairs so fast, he'd gone by the time I reached the door.

Oh, dear, poor Ash, I said to myself.

I went back to the table and tried to resume looking into flights to Venice, but was too distracted to focus. I got to thinking. What if there was some truth to Beth's story, after all when we told mum about Tom Bradley, she did sound a bit strange.

I was cross with Charley for bringing Beth to us. It was really uncool.

Yet again I was feeling that my day off was being hijacked by this Tom Bradley guy; I was seriously beginning to resent him – and he was nothing to me. How could some complete stranger have such a repeated impact on my day!

I calmed down and made a cup of tea. My travelling plans would have to wait. I stood at the window, holding my cup of tea. I looked down to the street below, one lane was still closed off but apart from some fire damage on the tarmac, you really wouldn't know there'd been a crash. As my eyes refocused onto the window pane, I could see tiny bits of black stuck to the glass. I put my cup down and went to the cupboard to get a cloth and cleaning fluid. I went back to the window and reached around to the outside window glass and rubbed the surface clean with the cloth. As I cleaned I started thinking back to what Beth had said. I stopped cleaning and paused for thought. *What if there was an element in truth in what she said?* After all, Tom Bradley had contacted Ash and said he had a family matter to discuss with him. But why contact Ash, why not Mum?

Suddenly I felt frightened. Was there some past in my mother's life of which we knew nothing? I had always prided myself on having an honest relationship with both my parents. I didn't know what to do, I felt at a loss. Should I go and see mum? What if there was some truth in what Beth had said, but dad was as in the dark as Ash and I were?

I had to sort this out. Either way I needed to know and put the record straight.

I phoned Mum.

"Mum, are you free?" I asked.

"I could be, why?" she replied.

"It's my day off, and it's not really gone to plan. I thought we could meet up. You always know how to cheer me up."

"Darling, of course. Come round and I will make some tea," she offered.

"No mum, I don't want to come round. Could you come here, or could we meet in town?"

Mum, went quiet. "Ok", she said hesitantly, as though she suspected something was up. She had already had a call from Ash this morning. If what Beth had said was true, she could be feeling nervous.

"Give me half an hour, I'll meet you in Chocolate Café, my treat," she continued.

"Aww Mum, love you. See you then." This was typical of Mum, whenever I felt down she knew exactly what to do to cheer me up. The Chocolate Café was the best place. It had the most amazing cakes and an incredible choice of drinks, all with added chocolate of course. I suddenly felt much happier and was really looking forward to seeing her.

I finished cleaning the window, it looked much better without the black spots on it. Cleaning the window had a very therapeutic effect. I got my things together and made my way into town. It was good to leave the house by the front door and not be faced with complete chaos. I felt empowered that I was regaining some element of normality and control.

The feeling was short lived however. As I made my way nearer to the Chocolate Café, I was reminded of the real reason for going there and meeting Mum. I was hoping, with fingers crossed, that she would tell me what I wanted to hear. To confirm what I knew to be true, that Beth had made a gross mistake and that our family's dignity would remain unscathed. Part of me did feel very guilty of the ordeal I was about to put my mother through. She really didn't deserve it. However, I had to put this rumour to rest. An element of doubt had been festering and I needed to end it quickly. Beth's words had made me angry, confused and irritated. I also felt cross with myself for giving it the tiniest bit of credence. Ash would be mad with me if he knew I was going to confront Mum. Was I making a huge mistake?

Before I knew it I'd arrived at the scrumptious Chocolate Café. It was housed in an old Tudor building with uneven floors, low black-beamed ceilings and rickety staircases. I loved it; it was quirky and fun. I'd arrived first, so I found a table and waited for mum. As I perused the menu, she walked in.

"Hello Dandie," she said smiling, as she sat down opposite me at the table. "How are you, rough day?"
"Haha, you could say that. It's really not how I'd expected my day off to be. Seriously I'd have had a much less stressful day had I gone to work!" I laughed.
"What are you having?" she asked. We each chose our very extravagant cakes and ordered drinks. We chatted over this and that, nothing really. I asked her about dad, told her a little about my day and that I'd met up with Ash, and she asked how he was. This went on for several minutes, then I took a deep breath.

58

"Mum, something really weird happened today," I almost smiled at myself at this understatement of events.

"Go on," she replied calmly, reassuringly.

"Mum… you know about the car crash today?"

"Yes," she replied without making eye contact, stirring her drink with a spoon.

"Well…you know Ash was expecting to meet one of the victims?"

"Yes," she replied, looking straight at me now, with a serious expression on her face.

"Oh, I really don't know how to say this…" I hesitated, unsure how to continue. I took a deep breath and blurted it out. "Mum, did you have a child and put him up for adoption?"

There I'd said it. I felt instantly awful, as though I'd betrayed my own mother. I suddenly felt a wave of self-hatred. *How could I ever have taken any notice of a complete strangers fabricated lies and present them to my mother?*

"Oh mum, I'm sorry, really I shouldn't have listened to gossip. I'm so sorry, please forget what I just said. Forgive me?" I pleaded.

Mum didn't say a word. I'd hurt her feelings, I felt so stupid. I wanted to rewind the last few minutes and delete them.

She reached out her hand to mine and held it tight.

"Dandie, darling…" she paused, her eyes were welling up.

"Mum?" I exclaimed. "Mum, you're frightening me."

"Dandie, there's something you should know," she paused again. I didn't want her to continue talking. How I wished right now that I had never called the meeting.

"No!" I said, angrily.

59

"Dandie, there was a child," she composed herself and squeezed my hand. She was such an elegant and calm lady. After a pause she continued. "A very long time ago, something happened…"

Chapter twelve

I sat in my favourite café opposite my mother, unsure what was going to come next. I almost didn't want her to continue, afraid of what I might hear. I wished I hadn't called this meeting. If only I could turn the clocks back, I would have gone to work today.

Mum sat calmly, but she looked scared. She was shaking and her hand still clasping mine, had become sweaty. I waited with apprehension of what she had to say.

"Mum, you don't have to continue," I said hurriedly. Rather than quietening her, this prompted her to speak up.

"I was very young, just fifteen. I was incredibly naïve and green..." She was not making eye contact with me, she was looking down at the table. "There was a party...a Halloween party." She paused, her voice, body, everything was trembling. "It was at a friend's house...we had gone there straight from school and spent hours dressing up, putting on make-up and so on." She smiled nervously. "It was fun dressing up, we were having a good time. There were four or five of us in the house. My friend, whose house it was, had invited some other people around. I wasn't expecting that, but it didn't matter. My friend's parents went out and left us all to it."

Mum was looking sad and very serious. I held her hand tightly. She wiped a tear from her cheek, and continued.

"Some boys turned up, I didn't know who they were. I don't know if they'd been invited or just gate-crashed...one boy started showing me some attention. I was flattered.

We were drinking and smoking, the music was loud. It's a funny thing to say, but because I was dressed up and wearing all this make-up, I didn't feel like me, I felt like I was someone else, if that makes sense?" She looked up at me, as though seeking reassurance. I nodded.

"This boy…he made quite a fuss of me, he kept getting me drinks, asking me to dance, cuddling and kissing me. It was nice, I was having a great time. The first boy to ever have taken an interest in me. I don't think my friends noticed, they were too busy partying."

Mum paused, let go of my hand and drank her drink, looking down at the table. I didn't know what to do, I felt incredibly uncomfortable, scared of what was to come. She looked up at me with sad eyes and again reached out her hand to mine. "I'm so very sorry, please forgive me," she pleaded.

"I love you Mum. Don't continue if you don't want to," I replied.

"No, you have a right to know," she said, sighing heavily. She withdrew her hand from mine and tightly crossed her arms. "This boy…he led me into a bedroom, it was really dark, I started to feel uncomfortable. He cuddled me and started stroking my hair. Suddenly it didn't feel nice anymore, it felt creepy and sordid, I don't know why. I told him I wanted to go out of the room, that I was scared of the dark…but he held me closer and told me not to be afraid, that he'd look after me. I felt reassured, and well, one thing led to another…" She took another long pause. "We spent the night together, but I couldn't sleep and left in the early hours and made my way home…" I looked at my mother in disbelief. "I felt very confused, of course I knew about sex, but I'd never been intimate with a boy before. I think the main problem Dandie, was that I didn't know this boy at all – I didn't even know his name. I felt as though he'd taken advantage of me. It wasn't the way I'd imagined it to be."

She drank some more of her coffee.

"Suffice to say, I never saw him again. I didn't tell anyone about him either. I don't know why, girls were always bragging about their sexual exploits, but somehow my experience didn't seem to warrant shouting about. Instead I felt embarrassed, ashamed even. Strange really," she said thoughtfully. "I just kind of pretended it didn't happen."

"I started to put on weight, I didn't really notice at first. I had taken to wearing unflattering loose clothing as was the fashion back then, so my body shape was hard to see. I was five-and-a-half months pregnant before anyone realised. I hadn't given it any thought that my periods had stopped, maybe I was in denial. My parents noticed and started asking questions. I hadn't told a soul about 'the incident'. I told my parents that it was a one night stand, and I didn't know the boy's name, which was basically the true story.
Anyhow, they took control, my parents. It was too late to have an abortion, so they kept me off school, with some health excuse, and went on to make the necessary arrangements for adoption. I didn't have a say in the matter. Really I didn't care. I didn't feel a bond for the baby, I felt more like I had a parasite living inside me which I was desperate to be rid of."
"Wow!" I exclaimed, shocked at what I was hearing.
"I went into labour prematurely, it's strange, but I don't even know how premature he was. I gave birth in hospital with my mother at my side, and the baby was taken away as quickly as possible. I didn't even see him. I think he was put in an incubator, but I'm not sure. After a couple of days

in hospital I went home. It was never spoken of again, ever."

"Does Dad know?" I asked,
"Yes," Mum replied, looking at me now, smiling. "It took me a long time to tell him. I was scared he'd judge me and leave. He is the only person I've ever told, apart from my parents. I'm not proud of what happened. It took me a long time to trust him and gain the courage to tell him, but I'm so glad I did. He really did turn my life around and brought me happiness I thought I'd never find, let alone deserve."
"And the boy, the father of the child, what of him?" I asked.
"No idea," she said, bluntly.
"Did he know about the child, did you ever see him again?"
"Nobody knew about the child, and no, I never saw him again."

"You know, it's funny Dandie, but I hear stories all the time through work of mothers who've given up their children, and it's different for every one of them. How they cope with the loss depends so much on circumstance but also very much on the support they receive. You see, I had no support, there was no one to whom I could speak. I was so young and naïve, I didn't really understand the long-term implications of what had happened and what I did. I wish my parents hadn't found out. I don't know how things would have ended up, but they were so black and white about it all, there was no discussion, it was simply a straightforward decision made entirely by what they considered to be the right way of dealing with it. I am absolutely sure that had they known sooner, they would have insisted I abort. Would that have been better? I don't know. In retrospect I think not, least because the boy had a chance and I like to think that I gave a couple somewhere the chance of happiness too."

I sat quietly for a while, struggling to absorb everything my mum had just told me.

"Did you ever think about the baby?" I asked. Mum hesitated.

"Yes, and no. I tried to block it from my mind. You have to understand Dandie, the only way I could move forward was to pretend it never happened. I pretty much went off the rails big time for a few years afterwards, filled with self-hatred and worthlessness. I really didn't care very much about anything, until I met Jim."

She took a deep breath. "When we got together and discussed having children, I was terrified, terrified that I wouldn't bond with any children we had, it took a lot of persuading. But when I fell pregnant with Ash, it was the most wonderful thing, I was so happy. I felt I'd been given a second chance, a forgiveness. I couldn't have imagined how wonderful it felt to be pregnant and give birth, it was unexpected because I hadn't felt like that before, not at all. After I had my children within a loving healthy relationship I did allow myself to think of the baby I'd given up. I have always felt incredibly guilty about it, but through having you lot it made me realise that at least I had given a childless couple the opportunity of being parents and that thought really helped me in the healing process. Someone had benefitted from my mistake, which gave me a huge amount of reassurance that I wasn't such a bad person."

We both sat in silence, contemplating all that had just been discussed. After a few minutes, mum looked up at me.

"Please don't judge me Dandie," Mum said nervously.

"As if!" I replied, shocked at the suggestion. "Mum, what happened to you was out of your control. You are in no way to blame, Jeez." I couldn't believe she even needed me to say it. I reached over to her to hug her.

"Do you think Tom Bradley is the child you gave up?" I asked tentatively. I didn't want to overstep the mark, but I had to know.
"Yes, I think he may be," she replied.

Chapter thirteen

After Mum's 'confession' I felt a mix of so many emotions, it was very confusing. I felt angry, protective, sad and helpless. I had always seen my mum as a strong, supportive and gentle person. Someone I could always rely on to be there for me, dependable. I had never viewed her as someone who was vulnerable. Someone with a 'past'.

We sat in silence for some time, mum was gazing out of the window and she looked so sad. I could tell that she would rather I had never known.

"Do you want to see him?"
She paused in thought, "I don't know, yes, I think I do."
She paused again. "He has a right to meet me doesn't he? I guess I always knew deep down, that he'd look for me."

Poor Mum I really did feel for her. She'd put her past behind her and built a new life with a new family. She was such a warm and loving person, to harbour such self-doubt couldn't have been easy. I was glad she'd told me what had happened, I just wish she'd told me before, so we could have had time to prepare for the inevitable. I think that was a mistake on her part, but hell, what do I know about what she went through?
I gazed at my mother in a new light, she seemed much smaller somehow, older and sad. I couldn't ever remember seeing her sad before, she was always happy and smiling.

"Dandie, I'm going to go now, hope you don't mind."
With that she reached over to me and kissed me on the cheek, then she paid the bill and left. I stayed sitting at the

table for a while. I watched her out of the window as she walked off down the road.

So many thoughts were racing through my head; I felt deeply sad, shocked and confused. I was also curious as to how Charley had worked out our relationship with Tom Bradley. I wondered how Ash would he react when and if, he found out? Should I now think of this Tom Bradley as some sort of relation?

I left the café and decided to ring Charley.
"Dandie, I'm so sorry," she immediately said on the phone.
"It was really uncool Charley!" I said to her crossly. "How on earth did you make the connection with my family anyhow?" I asked.
"Well Beth contacted me, she wanted a change of scene from the hospital, so I met up with her. She then told me that Tom was also meeting Ash Jensen, whom he believed to be a relation and told me all about being adopted and searching for his birth mother. I couldn't believe the coincidence, so I spilled that I knew you and things just escalated really quickly. She was desperate to meet you, saying that Tom had become obsessed with finding out about his past. I'm sorry, I just got swept up with the excitement of it all, and I wanted to help her. I didn't think."
"Really Charley, you could have forewarned us."
"I know. Beth's very persuasive you know."
"Don't care Charley. I'm your best friend."
"Is it true Dandie, could you be in some way related to Tom?"
I played it safe and told her that I didn't know. It was up to Mum now how we acted this out. I felt very protective of Mum right then.

"If you want to gossip with Beth, why not tell her about how you spent so much time with her boyfriend in Venice!" I suggested spitefully. It seemed a suitable moment to hang up.

Although it was late in the afternoon, the sun was still shining. I felt lost, not really sure what to do with myself. I didn't want to go home, too many bad things had happened there today. I found myself walking back towards the river. Our boat trip had been the absolute highlight of the day. I wanted to recapture some normality and happiness. As I got closer to the boathouse, I suddenly felt panicky. What if the same boatman was there? That could be awkward. I started to change direction and find another way to the river. As I walked along, deep in thought, a voice called out to me.

"Hello!"
I nearly jumped out of my skin. I looked up, it was the boatman from earlier!
"Um, hello," I said shyly.
"Sorry I didn't mean to frighten you. I'm walking this way too, do you mind if I join you?"
"No, not at all," I replied, slightly stunned.
"Did you enjoy your boat trip?" he asked.
"Yes, very much," I replied. I really didn't know what to say to him.
"Nice day for it," he continued.
"Yes, it is," I replied nervously.
"Funny that we should see each other again."
"Yes," I felt so self-conscious it was ridiculous. I just couldn't think of anything even vaguely intelligent to say to him. I couldn't believe that he was bothering to make conversation with me, but I was extremely happy that he was.

"My name's Ben, by the way," he said and reached out to shake my hand. I limply shook it, feeling myself blush.

"Dandelion, Dandie," I offered.

"Interesting name, I'll not forget that in a hurry."

"I hope not," I replied flirtingly and laughed awkwardly.

We continued to walk along the road together. He had a nice voice, it was deep but soft too. He spoke slowly and gently. It was very calming listen to. *Well this was unexpected that's for sure.* I was thinking. Seriously, guys never show me any attention. *Maybe he's just a player, and chats up all the ladies?* Hmm, I suddenly didn't feel so great about my circumstances.

"I don't make a habit of just talking to women, you know," he said, almost as though he had read my mind.

"I should hope not." Was all I could think of to say, feeling as though I'd been caught out.

"It's just that you have such a lovely smile, I couldn't pass you by without saying hello, it would've seemed rude."

I had to stop myself from giggling. I was incredibly flattered by his words.

"Thank you," I hesitated. "I'm glad you did," I continued and smiled at him.

He looked really pleased, turned away and smiled to himself. It suddenly occurred to me that he may be quite shy.

I didn't know where I was going, I simply continued walking along the pavement with Ben. He was great company, we weren't really talking about anything in particular, but it seemed so easy to talk to him. He made me laugh too, little anecdotes about the life of a boatman. I did bravely suggest that he was in a good position to pick up girls. He laughed it off and told me that generally the girls didn't notice him and anyway he had been in a long-term relationship for years, so it hadn't even occurred to him.

I didn't believe for one minute that girls hadn't noticed him, but was reassured that he had been in a long relationship so probably hadn't been looking.

He asked about Ash and seemed greatly relieved when I explained that he was my brother. I asked him about his long-term relationship. He told me that they had separated on good terms about five months ago. This was all very interesting I thought, but still didn't really flatter myself that he may be interested in me.

We came to a crossroads and he told me that he had to go. Before we parted though, he asked me if I would like to meet up with him sometime. I agreed and we swapped phone numbers. He crossed the road and smiled at me. I stood on the corner and suddenly realised that I wasn't exactly sure where I was. Feeling stupid, I turned and walked up a random road until I was out of Ben's sight.

Mobile phones are life savers aren't they? I found out where I was on the GPS and wandered back towards home, very much happier than I had been fifteen minutes earlier.

Chapter fourteen

Well, boatman Ben, who'd have thought! I chuckled to myself. He seemed like a cool guy to me, and I had his number, and he had mine, yay. I thought he may even like me a little bit. We would meet again.

I almost skipped all the way home, feeling like a smitten teenager. I couldn't stop myself from laughing out loud. What a roller coaster day of emotion this was turning out to be.

I had walked so far that I had to walk right through the town centre to get home. Even though it was late in the day, town was buzzing, surprisingly. I could hear a loud rhythmic drumming sound coming from up ahead. As I got closer all I could see was a huge crowd of people. The noise of the drums was so loud it literally pounded through my body. I squeezed through the crowd to get a closer look. I finally managed to get a view of the source of the music. It was amazing, there must have been twenty to thirty drummers and whistlers. The drums were harnessed around the drummer's bodies and they were all dancing down the street. The drums were all sizes, from huge to hand held, and the noise was incredible. The rhythm was hypnotic and as the band danced down the road, the crowds following them were all dancing in step too, you couldn't help but move to the beat. It was fabulous and the people loved it. We were all dancing in the street and it was great. The high-pitched whistles enhanced the excitement of the crowd.

I looked over and saw a familiar face, it was Jake.

"Jake," I yelled over at him, but he didn't hear. I squeezed my way through the crowd to him.

"Hey, Dandie, how are you?"

"Twice in one day!" I said to him. "Isn't this great, what's it all about?"

"No idea, Dandie, but they are fab! What are you up to?" he asked.

"Nothing much, just heading home."

"Fancy stopping off for a pint?" he asked.

"Yeah, why not. Great idea."

I felt so relaxed with Jake, there was no awkwardness between us at all. It was a purely platonic friendship and I think that's why it felt so comfortable. He was a lovely kind guy, and fun too.

We followed the band to the end of the High Street, stepping in time to the beats of the drums, then dived into the nearest pub.

"What you having Dandie?" Jake asked from the bar.

"Something incredibly strong Jake, I've had a crazy day!"

The pub was heaving but we managed to find a quiet nook to hang out in.

"Yeah, Jake, since I saw you earlier, the day just got crazier."

"Ah Dandie, you're a magnet for adventure," he replied teasingly.

"No, seriously Jake, you wouldn't believe the things that have happened today. I hardly believe them myself!" I went on to tell Jake most of the extraordinary things that had happened, with the exception of mum's story. We got on to the topic of boatman Ben.

"Ha ha, Dandie, I know Ben, Ben Stead," Jake said.

"No way! Jake, today has been totally full of mad coincidences, so I'm not surprised. But now you've told me you know Ben, spill."

It turns out Jake went to school with Ben. Ben's house had been the local hangout, on account of him having very liberal parents. Jake said he often crashed there after a heavy session. He had even had a brief fling with one of Ben's sisters.
"How come I've never met him before or heard you mention him?" I asked.
"I don't know Dandie, I guess I was older when I met you and was mixing with a different crowd. Don't see Ben much these days, bump into him at the odd gig or party. I think he was in quite an intense relationship with a girl called Alice for a long time. Don't think they went out much, went a bit middle aged if you ask me."

Well, I guess that explained why I hadn't come across him before. I was intrigued now to hear more about Alice. Jake couldn't really shine any light on her though, unfortunately on account of him not really knowing her as they didn't go out much. He did say that he'd heard she was quite controlling of Ben though.
"Hey Jakey!" a familiar voice called out. It was Ash.
"Ash, what are you doing here?" I asked him as he came and joined us.
"Mooching," he replied.
"Pint Jake?"
"Yep man," Jake replied.
"Kid sister?"
"Oi!" I replied, "But since you're offering, a double please."
"Well, what are you two up to?" Ash asked when he returned with the drinks.

"Drumming, dancing, gossiping, drinking – in that order," Jake responded.

"You know Jake, it would have made more sense if it had all been in reverse," Ash said.

"Reverse?" Jake asked.

"Yeah – you were drinking, so you started gossiping, which would lead to dancing because the gossiping would have got boring, and then having been dancing, it's an obvious progression to drumming – makes much more sense. Cheers!"

"Hey Ash, you remember the boatman?" I said.

"Boatman, umm, vaguely," he replied.

"Well, I bumped into him later in the day."

"Yeah?"

"Yeah, Jake knows him. He's pretty cool I think."

"Ohh, my kid sister has an admirer?" Ash said teasingly.

"Maybe," I replied, slightly coyly and slightly embarrassed. "And stop calling me 'kid sister'."

Ash suddenly turned more serious. "What the hell was that stunt by Charley earlier, how dare she!"

"Way out of line," I replied. I didn't want to talk about that here and now, especially as Ash had been drinking.

"What did she do?" Jake asked innocently.

"Not now," I said quietly to Jake.

"She brought some total stranger round to Dandie's place and started spouting off some bizarre rubbish about adopted children," Ash started.

"What?" said Jake, completely confused.

"Really, we'll talk about it later Ash, she didn't mean anything by it."

"Good job mum and dad don't know anything about it. Seriously Dandie, Charley needs use her head a bit better."

"Ash, shut up!" I said.

"Changing the subject completely Ash, Ben seemed really nice, I think we may meet up again, I hope so," I said.

"Aww, Dandie, you do deserve a nice guy in your life," said Ash.

"Ben's alright," confirmed Jake.

I would like to think that it meant something to Ash that I was interested in someone, and that someone was nice, but in reality I don't really think Ash gave it any thought at all. Girls literally threw themselves at him, he never seemed to have to make any effort, and was not a relationship type of guy anyway. So to expect him to be interested was probably a little too optimistic.

Still, Jake was interested and even better he could tell me a little bit about Ben. One of the many reasons Jake was such a good friend, it was a shame that there was no chemistry between us.

Chapter fifteen

Ash bringing up the subject of Tom Bradley again brought it all back. This guy was seriously starting to irritate me and I didn't even know him. I felt cross that one unknown person could have such a huge impact on my day.

The alcohol did have the effect of changing my perspective slightly. On the subject of mum in particular, I found myself looking at the situation from a very different angle. Tom would not have any idea, I guess, about mum's circumstances or how he came to be in the world. For him, he was simply searching for roots. I mean, why do people give up children for adoption? I suppose there could be any number of reasons. Whichever way you look at it, complex emotional issues are going to be lurking. I think it would be wrong to assume that all children put up for adoption are unloved, far from it, but the circumstances of the parents at the time of birth cannot be easy.

For the first time today I really felt for Tom Bradley. He had done nothing wrong; he was a complete innocent and yet I found myself resenting him without even knowing him. From what Charley had told me about Venice Tom, he sounded pretty cool, an interesting and nice guy. I gave out a big sigh. Ash was never going to be sympathetic towards Tom Bradley, I just knew it.

"What was that about?" Ash asked.
"What?" I replied, taken aback.
"You sighed."
"Oh, did I? Tired I think, it's been a hell of a day. So much for a relaxing day off."

"Ha ha, you'll have to have another day off to recover from today," Jake laughingly said.

"That's no joke Jake, I think you're right!" I added.

I decided it was time to leave. I made my excuses and left the boys at the pub. I was starting to feel hungry, and fancied a takeaway on the way home.

I wanted to find out more about Tom Bradley. I phoned Charley as I walked along the pavement.

"Charley, are you on your own?" I asked,

"Yes," she replied nervously.

"Sorry about earlier, I over reacted – but you were out of line. Anyhow, can I come round and see you?" I asked.

She seemed hesitant, but agreed. I bought some chips and headed to her place. It took ten minutes to get to Charley's, ten minutes of eating chips and mulling over all of today's events.

Charley lived in a cute little flat. It was all very retro in furnishings and accessories, a little like entering a time warp and being transported back to the 1950s. It didn't have the dreariness of the fifties décor though, it was kind of 1950s as seen through psychedelic technicolour. She even had a jukebox, her pride and joy, in prime position complete with florescent lights and forty-five inch vinyls. She was more organised than me and her pad reflected that. Everything was tidy and coordinated, but still interesting and quirky. I liked being in her place, it was more relaxing than my chaotic abode. In my flat things made places for themselves, and they sort of stayed where they were randomly placed. At Charley's everything was deliberately placed; even her writing desk was tidy. There were piles of paper, magazines and newspapers, but they were in organised tidy piles. You see, if I had been doing Charley's job the paper, magazines and newspapers would be scattered all over the floor, sofa, bed, table and kitchen. It would be impossible for me to find what I was looking for. It's probably why Charley has the job of a reporter and I don't, well one of the reasons anyhow.

"Dandie, I'm so sorry about earlier, it was really thoughtless of me. Beth is very persuasive you know and I just didn't think," Charley greeted me apologetically.
"Yeah, it was really uncool Charley, however..." I replied.
Charley looked at me expectantly for what was about to follow. I hesitated. I wanted to tell her about mum and Tom, but suddenly felt as though I was about to embark on act of betrayal.

"Have you got anything to drink?" I asked.
"Sure, glass of wine or bottle of beer?" she offered.
"Wine, please." I sat down on her sofa. "Your place is really nice you know, Charley."
She handed me a glass of wine, sat down next to me and waited. I could tell she was a reporter, she knew just how to get information out of people without pushing them. She had this way of making you feel like you should tell her what she wanted to know, as though you would be withholding information if you didn't open up to her.
"Blimey, you're good!" I said.
"What do you mean?" she asked innocently.
"Never mind." I took a sip of wine, it was red and it was nice. I suddenly realised just how much alcohol I'd consumed today, but then it wasn't any ordinary day and it washed the chips down perfectly.
"Tell me more about Tom Bradley," I asked.
"What do you want to know?" she replied.
"Everything you know." I said.
"Well, I had a long chat with Beth and she confirmed that Tom had been in Venice, so he is definitely Venice Tom."

"Wow," I replied, although we sort of suspected that already, it was a big deal to have it confirmed.

"Did you tell her?" I asked.

"Thought about it, thought better of it. Probably not the right time," she added.

"Charley, turns out there is truth in Beth's accusation."

"What do you mean?" Charley asked.

"I met mum… I think she could be Tom's birth mother."

Charley looked at me wide eyed.

"Go on," she said in a reassuring manner.

Part of me really didn't want to carry on, I felt disloyal to mum. On the other hand I really needed to offload this information, I needed to tell someone and Charley was my closest friend.

"Well it seemed that mum had an 'encounter' with a stranger when she was pretty young, and, well Tom was the result." I went on to tell her everything mum had told me.

"Your poor mother!" was all she came back with. We sat in silence for a few minutes and I felt sad and confused.

"It wasn't her fault, you know," I said, suddenly feeling as though I had to defend her.

"Dandie, you don't need to say that. Stuff happens, you know. It happens all the time. Sylvie is a wonderful woman and I don't think anyone could ever have a bad opinion of her. She was a victim of circumstance and that is that."

"So, how does she feel about the boy?" Charley continued.

"Tom Bradley?"

"Yes."

"Hmm, really not sure. She must have known he'd come looking for her, but I still think it's a big shock for her, for all of us."

"And what about the boy who made her pregnant, what happened to him?" Charley asked.

"I don't know. Mum implied she didn't even know who he was. I don't think he was ever held to account."

"Probably for the best. Poor Sylvia, wow!" Charley replied.

I felt relieved to have been able to talk about what had happened to mum, but I also felt as though I had opened a can of worms. Mum had kept this secret for nearly thirty years, and here I was spreading the word. Could I trust Charley to not let it go any further? I felt uncomfortable and disloyal. I don't think mum would appreciate me telling anyone her business, especially this.

"Charley, you mustn't tell anyone what I have just told you, please. Mum would be mortified if she knew I'd told anyone."

"Of course not!" Charley replied indignantly. "Does Ash know?"

"No, not yet." I replied.

"I've just had a realisation," said Charley. "Venice Tom is your half-brother!"

I laughed, "Yeah, maybe! Wow, how crazy is that!"

There was a knock at Charley's door.

"Who's that?" I asked nervously.

"Don't know," replied Charley. She got up and opened the door; it was Beth.

"Hi Charley, sorry, I just had to get away. I'm being a nuisance I know, but I feel twitchy with so many loose ends lying around." She had just returned from a hospital visit. Charley invited her in. She entered into Charley's living room and saw me.

"Oh, hello. You're here," she said, stating the obvious.

81

I looked at Charley, terrified she might share my confidence. She winked at me reassuringly.

"How is he?" I asked, genuinely interested. Everything had a new angle to it now.

"He's still out of it," Beth sighed. "I don't know if he's still unconscious or drugged up on painkillers."

I didn't know what to say to Beth. I didn't feel comfortable around her. She seemed angry, aggressive even. I was slightly intimidated by her. She looked petite and sweet, but emotionally she was hard and determined. She would make a good business woman I thought, maybe she was?

"What are his injuries?"

"I don't know, they say he has suffered 'traumatic brain injury' and has fractured his knees, but nothing life threatening. It's just maddening that I can't communicate with him. They say it could be days," Beth said, pacing. "Look, I'm sorry if I was out of line earlier, thought you knew. Maybe he got it wrong, I don't know. I'm just looking for answers right now."

I felt it was time to leave, I made my excuses and left Charley's.

As I walked homeward in the evening light, I suddenly felt very alone. Today had been overshadowed by the crash and I was really pissed about that. I would watch a film and try to finish off the day in a relaxing, chilled out way.

When I got home, there on the table was the info I'd collected about Venice. This reminded me of the happier things that had happened to me on this extraordinary day: the money, boatman Ben, planning a holiday. I focused on these happier thoughts. I'd had enough of today, it was time it was over. I went to bed.

Chapter sixteen

At 7am, the alarm went off. I put on my dressing gown, made a coffee and sat on the sofa to watch the TV. As I held my coffee in my hands, I felt very reassured that today I was going to go to work and it would be a normal routine kind of day with no unexpected surprises or excitement, thank you.

I got up and left the house, so far so good. I exited my house through the front door onto the street. Everything was back to normal. Both lanes of the road were open and full of the normal traffic, cars going to work, cars doing the school run, cars going shopping. Altogether too many damn cars! Anyhow, I didn't have a car so was catching the bus to work. The bus stop was just a few streets away, as usual there was a long queue. It was a bit of a lottery sometimes as to whether I actually made it on and got a seat. I was listening to some great funky music on my iPod and almost felt like dancing in the queue; I wondered if people would think that strange?

I was relieved to be at work. It seemed unusually relaxed. Sometimes routine was a good thing I decided. Boring is so underrated. There was nothing extraordinary about my job, it's fun, it's undemanding, the people are nice, the pay's rubbish, it's what I do most days from nine to five. It could be better, a lot better, but today I had no complaints.

I shared a desk with Jade, she's a bit flaky, but sweet.
"Hi Dandie, how was your day off?" Jade asked.
I laughed, "Not as relaxing as I had expected it to be. Started off with a car crash outside my flat, and kind of went downhill from there," I replied.

"Yep, that's why I don't take time off work," she replied matter-of-factly.

I looked at her blankly, but she was staring intently at her computer screen.

"Do you know, there are more stars in the sky than there are people on the planet?" she asked.

"You don't say!"

"Yep, straight up, says so here," she said pointing at the screen. I smiled to myself and felt grateful to be sitting next to someone today who was so trivial and undemanding. I knew I was not going to be challenged on anything.

"You do know that the planet earth is a microscopic dot in the universe don't you?" I asked.

"It's bigger than the moon," Jade stated triumphantly.

"Yes, Jade," I sighed, smiling. Had I come to work yesterday instead, how more simple and uncomplicated life may have been?

I got up to get Jade and me a coffee. A day of Jade talking about nothing was just the tonic I needed.

"You know I could be an astronomer," Jade said.

"Really?" I replied, surprised.

"Yeah, Mike says I'm always looking at the sky, drives him bananas. He's like 'what you looking at babe?' all the time."

"What are you looking at?" I replied, intrigued.

"The stars, doh! I love looking up at them, they're so pretty, sometimes they move, and I've seen so many shooting stars. Mike says they're aeroplanes or satellites, but that's just because he doesn't ever see them."

"Jade, you do surprise me."

She giggled proudly. I liked Jade, she was a 'what you see is what you get' kind of girl. Very young, I think she may only have been just eighteen, but sassy. She was already living in a flat with her fiancé Mike, a trainee mechanic. They had been together for about three years. She left school at sixteen with barely any qualifications, but already she had a permanent full-time job, a flat with a live-in boyfriend and was busy planning their wedding next year. Every weekend they had Sunday lunch with her parents at their local pub. She was probably going to be very successful. Her life seemed straight forward and uncomplicated. I had to admit to being just a little bit envious. There's a lot to be said for simplicity sometimes.

"Yeah, think I may do an evening class, I could do a TV show then, you know, like the big guy with the broken glasses," she continued.
"Broken glasses?" I asked, confused.
"Yeah, you know the one. He knows everything about outer space. Watched his programme as a kid."
"Haha, you mean Patrick Moore!" I exclaimed. "He didn't have broken glasses."
"Oh Dandelion, he did! I don't know why he never got them fixed, maybe he couldn't afford to," she said, quite convinced.
"Jade, he wore a monocle," I said.
"Ooh Dandelion, you are rude," she giggled.
"Jade, a monocle is a single corrective lens."

Jade looked at me confused; she cleared her throat and started fiddling with her pencil. She didn't have a clue what I was talking about.
I began to go into detail and explain how a monocle works and why Patrick Moore chose to wear one, but I realised

that she just wasn't getting it and it was probably simpler to change the subject completely.

"How are the wedding plans going?" I asked, straying back into safe territory.

"Oh, really well. Aunt Jane and Aunt Julie are coming over on Saturday and we're going to Maybeline's for dress fittings. Dandelion, my dress is so pretty; I feel like I've just walked out of a Disney film! It's this shiny, silky material, really nice, ivory colour."

She continued to talk for about ten minutes about every tiny detail of her multi-layered, corseted meringue wedding dress. Jeez it sounded horrific, but I just knew she would look great it in. Jade did look a little bit like a glamour model, with the clothes on, of course. But she had that kind of body shape and the way she wore her make-up and hair, big and over-done. She had a definite 'orange' skin tone, she always wore pale pink lipstick and blue mascara. Her hair was long and peroxide white, carefully curled with curling tongs. I dread to think how long it took her to get ready in the morning, and I thought it a little bit sad too, that someone so young, who was genuinely naturally quite pretty should spend so much time and effort creating a cake face.

"Dandelion, when are you going to meet a nice man? You're not getting any younger you know."

"Thanks for that Jade, I'm not that old you know! As it happens, I did meet a nice man the other day." Suddenly I had her full attention.

"Ooh, tell me more!" she said excitedly. I told her all about boatman Ben.

"Has he rung you yet?" she asked.

"Jade, this was only yesterday!" I protested.

"You can't hang about Dandelion. I bet he'll phone you tonight."

"I'm not expecting a call just yet."

Jade seemed disappointed.

"I could phone him later?" I offered, I felt as though I had somehow let her down.

"No, Dandelion, my goodness, you can't call him! He must call you."

"Why?" I asked, genuinely confused.

"Because it's up to the man to do the chasing," she said as if it were the most obvious thing in the world.

"Why?" I repeated.

"Really Dandelion, I'm beginning to see why you're single. You can't be seen to be desperate. The man must make the moves, he's the boss, he's in control. When he calls you, which he will, because let's face it, you're not bad looking are you, then you can be pleased to hear from him and it will go on from there."

Jade made me laugh and shocked all at the same time. Feminism and the women's liberation movement seem to have completely passed her by. Her naivety was sweet but so misguided. Her whole role in life was to be a wife, mother and possession to be shown off by Mike. It was strange though, that behind the scenes I knew that although she acted as though Mike was in control of their lives, that really the opposite was true. Jade ruled the roost totally, but she did it so cleverly that he didn't realise.

Her outlook couldn't be more polar opposite of mine, but I didn't mind. She was ok, she was strong and actually quite independent in her own way. Her values were questionable to say the least and she would probably never live up to her potential, but I'm not sure that really mattered. She amused me, and provided much-needed entertainment and light relief at work.

"I'll keep you posted Jade." She high fived me, and we concentrated on work.

Funnily enough, in the lunch break, I got a text from boatman Ben. I laughed, should I tell Jade and prove her right. No, I'd keep it to myself for now.

Boatman Ben asked me if I was free on Friday night. Wow, I was excited now. I couldn't quite believe that he texted me, that he was even a little bit interested in me. Well it certainly put a smile on my face. I texted back in the positive and waited to see how this would develop.

Chapter seventeen

The day at work was reassuringly uneventful. Jade kept me entertained with her pearls of wisdom, and the text from boatman Ben kept me smiling. At the end of the day I made my way home and sitting on the bus, staring vacantly out of the window at the mostly stationary traffic, my thoughts drifted back to Tom Bradley. I had not allowed myself to dwell too much on the things mum told me yesterday – too much to have digested until now.

I did feel a surprising connection with him. Not just because mum may be his birth mother, but also because he was probably Venetian Tom – my best friend's 'holiday romance' that never was, plus the fact that he had a meeting with my ex, Sol. It all seemed too fantastic to take in really. So many connections, not to mention the fact that his accident was right outside my house - creepy.

I hoped he was ok, really I did. I started to worry about mum too, it must have brought up a lot of really difficult memories for her. I decided to pay her a visit to make sure she was ok. I could get off at the next stop, buy her some flowers and have dinner at mum and dad's. I texted to pre-warn them of my plan.

I adore my parent's house; it's a really cosy, warm and welcoming home. An early Victorian red brick terraced house with two-storey bay window and a dormer window in the roof. It has wrought iron railings and a slightly unhinged gate. There is a small front garden full of wild flowers, and uneven tiles on the pathway up to the front door which is half-wood panelling and half-leaded glass. Inside, the house is spacious but chaotic. The chaos does have some sort of order to it. It is filled with objets d'art and piles of books and magazines. Every wall space is hung with framed paintings and posters.

There are lots of animals too; they have three cats, two dogs, a rabbit and some chickens in the very long, back garden. Mum also has a vegetable patch out there. The house has four bedrooms. Rose and my bedrooms are now studies for mum and dad, and Ash's room is the only spare bedroom. Our parents are hoarders so there's still lots of evidence of our childhood dotted around the place. There's always music and noise in the house. Radios are left on in rooms, music plays on the CD player. It has a lively atmosphere.

I knocked on the front door, but it was just out of politeness, as the door's always open. I turned the brass handle and let myself in.
"Hello," I shouted. Mum came running towards me and gave me a big hug.
"Come into the kitchen, I'm just cooking dinner." A few minutes later Dad came downstairs.
"Hello Dandie," he bellowed and gave me a big bear hug. "And what do we owe the pleasure of the most beautiful young lady in town?" he asked.
"Just thought I'd pop in and bring mum some flowers," I replied.
"Gorgeous they are too, you clever lady." He took them from me and put them into a vase. "Whiskey?" Dad offered as he poured himself a glass.
"No thanks Dad," I said hesitantly. I wasn't sure if Mum had told Dad about our meeting yesterday and was a little wary of bringing the subject up, but I wanted to know she was ok.

"Come with me to the front room, I have something to show you," Dad said, I looked up at Mum, she smiled back at me.

"Off you go, I've got cooking to get on with," she said.

I followed Dad into the front room. He put on some jazz music and then proceeded to show me some of his latest work. Dad is a larger than life person; he is big in stature and big in personality, and loud. He is enthusiastic about everything, and good to be around. His positivity is infectious.

As we sat next to each other and he showed me his latest works and commissions, he quietly turned to me and said in a very uncharacteristic serious tone.

"Mum told me about the conversation you had yesterday. Are you ok?"

"Yes, dad," I replied. "Shocked, but ok. How is she?"

"Sylvie was very upset yesterday. I guess we knew this day would come, I think I was more prepared than she was." He paused, "She feels so much guilt, poor thing. I don't think any of us will ever really know what she went through. She was up all night last night."

"Poor Mum. How are you Dad?" I asked tentatively.

"It didn't happen to me, and it happened before I knew her. She didn't tell me for a long time, years in fact. When we first got together I couldn't understand why she was so distant, I thought she didn't like me," he laughed. "When she told me it was a relief in a funny way, because her behaviour suddenly made so much more sense. She had so little self-confidence and self-esteem, I couldn't understand it. Seriously, your mother was and still is, the most attractive and wonderful woman I ever had the fortune to meet. We built our lives together and it's something that we don't dwell on or pay much attention to. Now this has happened and it's really up to Sylvie how she moves forward with it. She is worried about the boy being in hospital, but at the same time has mixed feelings about meeting him."

"What should we do dad?" I asked.
"You're too sweet Dandie, all we can do is stand by her. Let her take the lead."
He took my hand and smiled reassuringly at me.
"She's got us to support her."
"What about Ash, Dad, do you think he should know, and Rose?"
Dad shrugged. "I don't know Dandie, let me deal with Ash and Rose. Right now we have a gastronomic delight being prepared in the kitchen and we have neglected the cook for long enough." He grabbed my arm and led me back into the kitchen, but before we entered he turned to me and said, "Don't worry Dandie, I would never let your mother be upset."
Aww Dad; he always had a way of making everything alright.

After dinner, Mum, Dad and I all sat in the front room. Dad drinking his whiskey, Mum and me a glass of wine. After an hour or so of, mostly Dad, talking and laughing about this and that, Mum suddenly interjected.
"I want to visit Tom Bradley," she said quietly.
Dad and I smiled at each other.
"Ok darling," Dad replied.
"Jim, I would like to see him. I have to know he's going to be ok. I would like to look at his face…I never saw his face you know," she said introspectively. "Do you think I have the right?"
"Sylvie, of course you have the right. He wants to see you, he searched for you. We shall visit him tomorrow, I'll find

out what the visiting hours are," Dad replied reassuringly, giving her a hug.

Mum didn't answer, or make eye contact with either of us, she just sipped from her glass of wine. I thought how brave she was.

"If you want me to come too, I will," I offered.

Mum looked at me and smiled; she reached out for my hand and gently took it. "That would be lovely Dandie, thank you."

I don't know what she was thanking me for, but I was also intrigued to come face to face with Tom Bradley.

I left my parents stuffed, wined and happy. I felt apprehensive but also excited about the possibility of a meeting with Tom Bradley. It seemed inevitable that we would meet at some point, so why wait? I did worry about the effect it may have on my Mum and am forever grateful that my Dad is such a tower of strength.

Chapter eighteen

On the way home I reflected on my parents' loving relationship. I really hoped that one day I would be as happy as they were, and meet a really genuine and caring man who would love me unconditionally. They were sweet, comforting thoughts.

On Thursday morning I woke feeling refreshed and ready for the day. I was looking forward to my undemanding day in the office and the superficial conversation I was inevitably going to have with Jade.

The doorbell rang. Coffee in hand and clothed in my dressing gown I went to the intercom to see who it could be so early in the morning. To my surprise it was my sister, Rose. I let her in; my relaxed state of mind suddenly replaced with anxiety. *Oh boy, what does she want?*

"Dandie!" she exclaimed matter-of-factly.
"Rose," I replied reticently.
Rose barged her way into my flat. She was wearing a suit and high heels and looked as boring and conventional as hell. Her hair was tightly tied back in a bun and her make-up was severe. She looked ten years older than me and she was my kid sister. *How can I be related to you?* I thought to myself.

"So!" she exclaimed, making herself at home.
"So?" I replied, confused by her visit. "Why are you here?"
"Seems things have been going on," she started.
Things? There have been a few things in the last couple of days, so I was intrigued to know which one she was referring to.

"Elaborate Rose, by the way…hello and how are you?"

"Skip the trivialities Dandelion, jump to the point," Rose demanded.

"I would if I had any idea what you are going on about," I answered. Rose really was lacking in any social graces.

"Look Dandelion, I don't have much time. I've been hearing rumours that you were witness to a car crash."

I looked at her blankly.

"What did you see and what did you say to the police. If either of the victims die, your statement could be used against you. I can get you a good lawyer; I think we should make an appointment now. Right when is your lunch break?"

I almost dropped my mug of coffee in disbelief.

"Rose, it's getting late, I have to get ready for work. Let yourself out." With that I left her in the front room, went into the bathroom and began running a bath.

"Dandelion, you are so naïve, it'll get in all the papers. Is that what you want?"

"You know where the front door is, right?" I shouted from the bathroom.

I told you she was living in a parallel universe didn't I? All Rose could think of was herself and her 'reputation'. Of all the things to worry about right now, my name in the papers as an innocent witness to a crash did not even register and never would. Besides in 'the real world' it just wouldn't happen. Rose's impromptu visit did make me think about how she might react if she found out about Mum and Tom Bradley, which did worry me.

I decided to walk to work today; I was running late due to my 'lovely' sister's visit, but time wise I don't think there was much in it, the bus was always so slow anyway. As the walk to work was pretty much along the same lines as the bus route, I could always catch it on the way if I needed to. It was quite a walk, but I needed to let off a bit of Rose frustration. Our parents are so gentle and kind and Ash and I get along so well, so I just couldn't fathom Rose out. Maybe it was youngest child syndrome, you know how they say that the youngest is overindulged and spoilt. Maybe she resented the relationship between me and Ash, which made her so mean. I don't know, not sure I care very much. It was a shame though.

As I walked swiftly to work, I wondered if Ash would be up and about yet; I gave him a ring.

"Hi Dandie, why have you woken me up?"

"Oh, sorry Ash, just had a visit from Rose."

"Yay, so you get to wake me up and piss me off at the same time, thanks!"

"I know, I'm so cross I'm walking to work to calm down. She really has a warped view of life you know."

"Yep!"

"It was great to see you the other day, Ash," I said,

"You too twinkle toes. Now can I go back to sleep?"

"Yes, maybe we could meet up again soon?"

"Sure," he replied and hung up.

It was another beautiful sunny day, and having contact with Ash made me feel happy again, restoring faith in my family. In a way I wished that Ash knew about Mum's past, I could have done with talking to him about it, but it wasn't my place to tell him.

A few minutes after talking with Ash, my phone rang, it was Sol.

"Sol!" I said, surprised to hear from him.

"Hi, can you talk?" he asked.

"Sure, I'm walking to work. How are you?"

"I'm good, I just wondered if you knew anything more about Tom Bradley, how he is?"

"Sorry Sol, I don't know anything."

"Ok, long shot I guess. Just feeling a bit weird about the fact that the only reason he was coming here was to meet up with me, you know, if he hadn't arranged the meeting, he wouldn't be in hospital."

"Sol, don't beat yourself up about it. Anyhow, it seems Tom Bradley was coming to town for other reasons than meeting up with you. Really, it's not your responsibility." I tried to reassure him but he sounded pretty down.

"I guess, it's just shaken me up a bit, I do feel responsible. Never mind, eh?" Sol paused, dragging on a cigarette, "How about coming to that gig I told you about?"

"Maybe, who's the band?" As I was walking and talking to Sol, I noticed a cyclist riding alongside me in the road, he seemed to have slowed down to my walking pace. I turned to look who it was and was stunned to see it was boatman Ben.

"Sol, I'll get back to you, I've got to go. Listen, don't fret ok. I'm sure the guy'll be fine. Bye." I hurriedly hung up and turned to Ben who was still cycling alongside me.

"Hello," I smiled at him.

"Hi, do you mind if I join you?"

"No, not at all." I answered, slightly awkwardly. This was turning out to be a morning of encountering unusual people. I was very pleased to be bumping into Ben.

"I don't normally see you walking along here," he said.

"No, I usually get the bus." I really didn't know what to say to him. I didn't want to say anything uncool, but at the same time felt that I just couldn't help it.

"Where're you going?" I asked, not being able to think of anything else to say.

"Off to set up the boats," he replied.

There was an uncomfortable silence which seemed to last forever. Then, typically, we both spoke at once.

"It's nice to see you..." I started at the same time he said, "About Friday night…"

We both laughed nervously. Jeez, I was acting like a teenager!

Ben stopped and stood in front of me. I stopped too and faced him.

"Dandie, I know we don't know each other, at all, but I would like to spend some time getting to know you, if that's ok with you?"

Ok with me? Was he kidding, I couldn't think of anything better. I literally couldn't believe this was happening to me. I wanted to grab him and hug him and leap around in some crazy dance. I didn't think that would go down too well though, so I tried very hard to compose myself and took a deep breath.

"Yeah, that sounds good to me", was the best I could come up with. *Why me?* I asked myself.

"So," he said getting even closer to me and touching my hand, "I was thinking, tomorrow night. I could come and pick you up and take you out?"

"Ok," was all I could say. I was just happy to be standing there touching hands.

"About 8pm?"

"Yes." I replied as all thoughts of being cool had completely diminished. I told him my address. He was going to come round and take me for a drink. He had to go but as he left he kissed me gently on the cheek, then got back on his bike and cycled off.

I just stood still on the spot for a few seconds. *Ok, what just happened?* I smiled to myself. Roll on tomorrow night, newsflash world: Dandelion Jensen has a date, hell yeah!

After an eventful and very brisk walk, I made it to work, admittedly fifteen minutes late, but I was sure that I could make that time up at the end of the day, or in my lunch break. Seriously, I didn't care.

Chapter nineteen

I found out during the day that Tom Bradley had regained consciousness. I wasn't sure how I felt about that. Obviously I was really pleased for the guy that he was on the road to recovery. However, it also meant that he was able to communicate, and that could open a whole can of worms.

I did have a little chuckle to myself, momentarily you understand, at the thought of Beth and Charley at his bedside at the same time – that alone would probably blow his mind. Although thinking about it, it was probably unlikely to happen.

As I left work that evening I was met by a surprise visitor outside.
"Hi Ash, this is a surprise! I didn't even know you knew where I worked," I said to him.
"Of course I know where you work, I was just passing, thought you might want a lift?"
"Really?" I said, unconvinced. "What are you after?"

We walked to his car with general chit chat exchange. When we got into his car, Ash said quietly.
"I met Dad today."
"Oh?" I replied, sensing what was coming.
"He told me about Mum." With that Ash punched the dashboard of the car.
I turned to look out of the window; I really didn't know how to react. Ash could be a bit unpredictable and fiery. I wasn't scared of him, I just had no idea what was going to happen next. Ash very much acted on instinct, in a kind of primeval way.

"How long have you known?" he asked me.

"A day or two," I replied. "Ash, it was a long time ago."

Ash got out of the car and slammed the door after him. He paced around outside, dragging heavily on a cigarette.

I just sat in the car and waited for him to calm down. I anticipated that it could be a while. I sort of wished Ash hadn't picked me up, I could be half way home on the bus right now instead of sitting in the car park just outside work. *Cheers for that, Ash.*

After waiting for about five minutes, I took a deep breath and got out of the car.

"Ash, are you taking me home, or should I catch the bus?"

"Is that all you can think about?" he said to me accusingly.

I walked up to him and stood beside him; I didn't really know what to say, so I kind of clumsily stated.

"Mum's news is a bit of a shock to be sure, but it's not the end of the world, in fact it's a new beginning isn't it?"

He didn't reply.

"Come back to the car, Ash," I said softly to him. He shrugged me off, strutted over to the wall of the car park and began kicking it.

"Ash, pull yourself together, you're going to hurt yourself. Why are you so cross? Now, please get in the car. Let's drive out of town, go to a country pub and sit down and talk about this," I pleaded with him to get back in the car.

Other people were leaving work and getting into their cars. I could see them all looking at us, not quite sure what was going on. I needed to get out of there.

Eventually Ash made his way to the car.

"I'll drive," I offered, taking the keys as I got into the driver's seat.

We drove out of town. Ash was silent but I could tell he was still agitated.

"What did you say to Dad?" I asked with some trepidation.

Ash took a deep breath and sort of huffed, "I dunno, I asked lots of questions, Dad couldn't really answer any of them."

I didn't have any answers either.

"All I can say Ash, is that it didn't happen to us; all we can do is be there for Mum. This must be pretty hard for her facing up to her past. It was inevitable that it was going to happen one day. I just wish she'd told us about it sooner, I can't understand why she didn't."

Ash didn't answer, he was still huffing and puffing like a bull preparing to charge.

"You know what Dandie, I hate this guy Tom Bradley already!" exclaimed Ash.

"Now that's a bit unfair – I admit, he's not been very convenient, but none of this is his fault. Really I feel quite sorry for him, he is an innocent in all this," I replied. "Ash I don't know why you're so cross. It was such a long time ago, and she's rebuilt her life which let's face it, can't have been easy."

"I guess I'm just really, really pissed that someone could have got Mum into a situation like this. What happened to the pimple head who did this to Mum, was he never held to account?" Ash asked.

"I have no idea. It's all a bit irrelevant now isn't it? Seriously Ash, I think you're focusing on the wrong things right now." I was beginning to lose patience with Ash, he was acting like an over-protective big brother now – *jeez, what would he be like if it had happened to me?* The thought made me shudder.

"Maybe," Ash replied.

We arrived at a lovely pub, The White Hart, very 'olde worlde' in the middle of a wood with a stream running alongside. The ceilings were low inside and I think it was at one time a coaching inn. It had a large cobbled courtyard outside. I bought Ash a pint and myself an orange juice. Sitting at a table by the window surrounded by horse brass, harnesses and other such paraphernalia, this was not where I was expecting to be at 6pm on a Thursday evening.

"Shall we get some food while we're here?" I suggested.

"Food, yeah why not flower?" Ash replied vacantly.

"Weed," I replied.

"What?"

"Dandelion is a weed, not technically a flower."

Ash looked at me stunned for a second, then broke out into slightly hysterical laughter.

"Ash, it wasn't that funny!" I said, feeling foolish.

"Oh Dandie, I couldn't wish for a better sister," he gave me a hug.

"Thanks," I replied, slightly surprised and confused. At least he seemed to have cheered up a bit. I put it down to the beer.

"Poor Mum, she was little more than a child, Dad said," Ash said.

"I know, I can't begin to think what she must have gone through, and to not tell anyone either. She was so ashamed, I think she thought it was somehow her fault."

"So no one knew, are you serious? No friends, her parents, no one?" Ash asked in disbelief.

"Don't think so, but I think her parents did, eventually," I replied.

We both sat in thought for a few seconds. I ordered some food for both of us.

"We need to be there by Mum's side, to show her that we love her and what happened was out of her control. It could be a good thing, you know, meeting Tom Bradley. She must have been curious about him. He's conscious by the way," I said. "Does Mum know Dad talked to you?"

"I don't know, I guess so," Ash said.

"Don't let her know you're cross, she could take it the wrong way and think you're blaming her."

"How could she think that?" Ash said, shocked.

"I don't know Ash, I don't know anything, I'm just saying, be careful. We don't want to upset her even more do we?"

"No, of course not. Another pint should do the trick."

I was hugely relieved that Ash seemed to have calmed down, but I was not convinced that was the end of his smouldering.

Ash and I ended up staying in The White Hart until almost closing time. I told him about my upcoming 'date' with Ben and he seemed genuinely pleased, which was sweet. I didn't think he'd be interested or care, so I was touched.

I drove Ash home and parked his car back at mine, he could collect it tomorrow. I was glad that Ash knew about Mum, but was unsure about how things may develop. Right now, though I was ready for bed and hopefully, a good night's sleep, after all I had a hot date tomorrow.

Chapter twenty

Friday. Where did the week go?

"Hey Jade, guess what I'm up to tonight?" I said as she brought me over a coffee and sat down at our desk.

She put the drinks down, sat down and gave me her full attention, as though she were anticipating some life-changing announcement.

"I'm all ears," she said expectantly.

"Well," I said, feeling suddenly a little shy and embarrassed. "I'm going out with Ben, the boatman."

"Yay, I knew he'd phone you, there you go, didn't I tell you?" Jade said excitedly and 'high fived' me triumphantly. "Where are you going, what time are you meeting, what are you wearing? I'm so excited for you!"

I felt as though I'd just received an onslaught of happy dust. I wasn't sure which question to answer first.

"How are you going to wear your hair Dandelion? Do you want to borrow my tongs? We could put up on top like so."

My hair was bobbed, so there wasn't a lot of it, or much you could do with it. That didn't stop Jade though, she proceeded to play with my hair like an over enthusiastic hairdresser.

"Jade, this is not the first date I've been on you know."

"I know, Dandelion, but it's been a while hasn't it? You're bound to be a bit rusty, a bit out of touch. Don't worry we've got all day. So, what are you wearing?" she repeated.

She somehow made me feel as though I were a middle-aged spinster.

I was under the impression we were in the office to work, obviously Jade didn't see it the same way. She immersed herself into the role of make-up artiste extraordinaire and produced a huge bag of beauty products, brushes and sponges. The thing is that I'm actually very comfortable with my 'look', and didn't share Jade's 'Barbie doll' role model. I wouldn't say my face was entirely natural looking, but compared with Jade's make-up application, I was positively naked.

"Jade, back off. I can do my own face, thanks," I resisted.
"Are you sure, Dandelion? You must make an impression, you don't want him to forget you do you?" she replied.
"Ok, Jade, if you must know, I am going to wear a pretty full-skirted knee-length dress, and red shoes. Now can we move on?"
"Not bodycon?" Jade asked, disappointed.
"No Jade, not bodycon!"
She was obviously unimpressed with my outfit choice, but seemed to have got the message to lay off. I felt bad as she was so excited for me. For a moment there I think she thought she had a full-size doll to play with. I felt I'd burst her bubble a bit, but really I couldn't let her carry on, I'd have ended up looking like a clown, and that would have blown my date for sure.

Jade was easily distracted thankfully, so the conversation quickly moved on to Mike. I felt for Mike, I really think he left his mother and moved in with a mother substitute. Jade totally ruled his world, she prepared all his meals for him, she told him what to wear every day (no surprise there), and she also made his social arrangements. Every day was mapped out for him. He did have his own social life with his friends, the football, the pool at the local, but the timings and meetings were all subtlety controlled by Jade. I don't think he minded, actually I'm not sure he was even aware how much she was controlling his life. It was done in a loving and caring way though, she was not sinister or malicious; she wanted him to be happy in life, but she needed to organise it for him. Maybe he wasn't capable of organising it himself, but from the outside it did look very much as though she mothered him totally.

Jade had their whole lives planned out: the wedding, when the first child would come along, how many children there were going to be, their names, Mike's career plan. I had to hand it to her, her organisational skills were impressive. If she had channelled her energy into her own career path I have no doubt she would be very successful and independent, but that wasn't her aim. She saw herself very much in the support role. Fair play to her.

The day dragged by, I was excited about seeing Ben in the evening and there was only so much Mike adulation I could take; I was suffering saccharine overload.

The working day finally came to an end. I nearly ran out of the building with excitement. I had a few hours to grab some food and change. I also had to stop off at the ATM and get some money at some point too.

I found sitting on the bus very stimulating and thought provoking. Staring blankly out of the window, my mind would often drift into deep thought. I started to worry a little about the evening. I didn't know boatman Ben at all really, and yet I had committed myself to an evening with him, alone. What if I found we had nothing in common after all? Worse, still, what if he turned out to be weird, or boring. Then I remembered the things Jake had told me about Ben, and felt much more relaxed and positive again. I slouched down comfortably on the bus seat and the smile returned to my face. Bring on the date, I was ready.

When I got back to the flat I quickly did a tidy up and vacuum, made myself some food and blasted some music out of the speakers, very loudly. All to do now was get changed, made up and enjoy a glass of wine. I looked in the mirror, was pleased with what I saw, raised a glass to myself and told my reflection that Ben was a lucky man to have me as his date.

Eight o'clock came and Ben rang the doorbell. He was very punctual, good job really because the longer I waited for him the more nervous I became. I really wasn't very confident with this dating malarkey. I buzzed him in and he made his way up to the flat.

"Come on in," I said shyly. He came in carrying a bottle of vodka.
"Pre-drinks," he said, almost excusing himself.

Chapter twenty one

I fetched some glasses for the vodka and we sat down on the sofa next to each other. Ben poured out the drinks.

I looked at Ben sitting there on the sofa next to me and couldn't quite believe he was real. He was dressed casually in jeans, long sleeved t-shirt, and jacket. He was slim build, not too skinny, he had a bit of muscle, I suppose he'd have to really working with heavy boats all day. His colouring was quite dark, I guess again as a result of working outdoors all day. He had short dark hair and a bit of a quiff. His eyes were big and dark, he had large sideburns but otherwise was clean shaven. He had very kissable lips and a lovely smile, good teeth too. He was about five ten in height at a guess, but he had long, slender legs. *Hmm kissable lips,* I thought to myself.
"Tell me a bit about yourself," he said to me. I felt suddenly alarmed, having drifted off into thoughts of kissable lips.

"Me, oh, umm. There's not much to tell really. I'm 23 years old, I have a lovely brother and an incredibly dull sister. I have the most amazing parents in the world and a cat called Marmalade, who lives with two other cats at my parents on account of the fact that my flat doesn't allow pets. I have a great bunch of friends, would love to travel and am planning a trip to Venice. Oh and the last few days have probably been the strangest of my life!"
"Wow, I'm not sure I can match that," Ben replied, smiling.
"Try," I said, smiling back at him.
"Ok, my name's Benjamin Stead. I have three sisters, no brothers, two older sisters, Polly and Bella, and one younger, Issy. I am 25 years old. I have been working on

the boats for around four years and it's the best job, it doesn't even feel like work. I basically run the place which is pretty cool. I used to live in a big old rambling house with my fam, it was a bit of a party house. My parents split up and sold the house, just before it fell down if you ask me. Mind you they sold it for a song! Wish I'd been able to buy it off them; I had some great memories and lots of awesome times were had there."

"Yeah, I heard stories about your house. You know my friend Jake."

"Jake. Jake who?" Ben asked, but before I could answer, he continued, "That house was crazy! My parents, Vincent and Jan, bought it a long time ago, but they were never very happy with each other. Between you and me, I think they only stayed together because of us kids. Didn't really do us any favours because they were never like a 'couple', they led completely separate lives and we were pretty much left to our own devices. They didn't care what went on in the house, they didn't really care much for the house at all. It was never looked after, decorated or fixed when things broke. I think they resented it really. It had become a poisoned chalice for them. When they first bought it we were all young, dad had a really good career, plus they'd just inherited a large amount of dosh. I think they got carried away with the grandeur of the place and bought it without much thought. Anyhow, slowly over the years they lost interest in it, each other and us really. They had begun living separate lives, having affairs ... you get the picture.

We didn't mind though, being teenagers with free reign of a rambling old pile and parents who didn't care what we were getting up to, seriously it couldn't have been better for us. Well, so we thought then. Looking back I think maybe a bit of parental guidance would have been a good thing. Anyhow that was all a long time ago. I'm happy to say that both my parents have moved on to happier places. My dad is living in a flat in London with his new wife and their two young children, and mum is living in a cottage in the Lake District with an eccentric artist called Randolph!"

"I'd heard about the goings on in your house from Jake."

"There were good times, good memories. Pretty wild!" Ben said reflectively. "So, you're planning a trip to Venice are you? I've never been but it's one of those places on everyone's bucket list isn't it? I've heard it's very smelly though."

"Really? I've not heard that. I just think it is the most romantic place in the world. My friend Charley has recently come back from a job out there. I could listen to her stories for ever. I'm planning my trip at the moment and hope to be going out there soon, in the next few weeks, and literally can't wait!" I said excitedly.

We sat on the sofa drinking vodka, listening to music and chatting and laughing for hours. He was lovely to talk to, so easy, relaxed and really interesting. He had a lovely deep soft voice that was so gentle and calming. I felt I could say anything to him and knew he wouldn't judge or criticise. I was so used to Ash trivialising things I said that I'd come to expect it from a guy, so it was refreshing to be taken seriously for a change.

We seemed to have so much in common too; we liked the same music, shared the same sense of humour, and liked the same films and books. It all seemed a little too good to be true. I was happy and having a lovely time.

The next thing I knew it was 3am, we'd drunk all the vodka and hadn't even made it out of the flat. We'd got so carried away with messing about, laughing and having fun. We were on the sofa together, Ben sitting upright and me lying with my head on his shoulder, his arm around me. I could have just fallen asleep, I felt happy and secure.

He looked at his watch.

"I've got to go Dandie, I have to get the boats ready in a few hours," he said apologetically.

"Oh, you're leaving?" I asked, surprised. I could have stayed on the sofa all night, or better still I thought he could share my bed.

"Yep, thanks for a great evening," he said as he stood up to put his jacket on. I stood up next to him; I felt a bit disappointed. I didn't want him to go.

He came up close to me and held me in his arms, then kissed me passionately on the lips.

"You can stay," I offered.

"Another time," he replied, smiling. "See you soon?"

"Yes," I replied.

He let himself out of the flat and I just stood frozen to the spot. I was confused; I thought he might have stayed the night with me. I felt a bit sad as we'd had such a nice evening. I pulled myself together, turned the music and lights off and made my way to bed.

As I lay in bed, I reflected on the evening I had shared with Ben. I really liked him and I think he liked me too, but I had to admit to being really confused by his sudden exit. Maybe he was just a genuinely nice guy? Did they still exist in the twenty-first century? Surely not.

Whatever, I had one of the best evenings for a long time, so for the time being I'd just hang onto that thought and see what tomorrow brought; it was Saturday and I didn't have to get up early, result!

Chapter twenty two

In deep sleep I was having an intense dream. Ash and I were floating down a river, the current was getting stronger and stronger; we were trying desperately to get to the riverbank and safety, when a huge log appeared alongside me. I shouted to Ash to try and reach it, but he couldn't hear me amongst the noise of the crashing water. I reached out and grabbed hold of the log, all the time calling out to Ash. I could hear a faint buzzing noise and as I tried to secure my grip on the log the buzzing noise got louder and louder; I looked around to see where it was coming from, but the sound of the water was distorting my sense of direction.

Then I recognised the noise, it was my phone! I woke up startled and confused; my phone was ringing next to my bed. I reached out to grab it, caller id – Charley.
"Hello Charley," I said, panting.
"You ok?" she asked.
"Yeah, sorry, just woke up. Was having an intense dream. What time is it?"
"Around 11am, sorry, did I wake you?" she replied.
"Don't worry, you did me a favour, I think I was about to drown! How's tricks?"
"Drown? Haha, don't feel so bad about waking you now," she laughed. "What are you up to today, fancy meeting up?"
"Yes, sure. Come over," I said, still struggling with reality versus dream.
We arranged that she would pop over in an hour to give me enough time to get up and wake up.

As I sat on the sofa cradling my morning coffee, I was looking forward to seeing Charley, and I was very happy reflecting on my evening with Ben. Remnants of the previous night were still around me in the living room; the glasses, and the empty bottles. Reminders of an evening well spent. I giggled smugly to myself. *I had an admirer, me! Little old Dandelion Jensen.* I had a lovely evening with boatman Ben and was really looking forward to seeing him again. We got on so well; he made me laugh and we didn't once talk about the whole Tom Bradley craziness which seemed to have dominated my week. The evening with Ben had been a breath of fresh air, refreshing and calming. Just the tonic I needed. I was glad that he hadn't stayed over too, somehow it seemed respectful. I know that sounds really old fashioned and out dated, but it was unexpected and that was cool.

Having reflected on the previous evening and realised that I was not in mortal danger of drowning, I got up and ready for Charley's arrival. Bang on time she rang the doorbell, I buzzed her up.

"Come on in," I offered, standing at the door.
Charley came in, holding a bunch of flowers which she handed to me.
"Are these for me?" I asked surprised.
"Yes, thought you deserved them."
"Aww, thanks doll," I replied and gave her a kiss on the cheek. "Come on in, sorry about the mess."
Charley looked around, "What did you get up to last night?" she asked intrigued.
"Only boatman Ben came over," I replied coyly.
"No way!" Charley replied excitedly, "Do tell,"

"Nothing to tell really, we just had a really great evening. Charley, we got on so well, we didn't even get around to going out!"

"Rock on Dandie!"

I continued to talk to Charley about the previous night and how nice it had all been, then we got onto the subject of Beth and Tom Bradley.

"How is he?" I asked.

"Well he's now totally conscious, but he can't walk because of the fractured knees. They've put them in casts."

"Have you been to visit him yet?"

"No, but Beth's still with me and goes to visit a couple of times a day."

"She's committed!" I exclaimed.

"Yes, they seem like a tight couple," Charley said thoughtfully.

"So, what do you think about Venice now?" I asked.

"You know what, Dandie. Tom never made a pass at me, I really think I was just reading things into our relationship which weren't actually there. He didn't do anything wrong, I just misinterpreted him."

"Really?" I said, unconvinced.

"Anyway, he's going home soon."

"Is he?" I said. I was suddenly a bit shocked. I don't think Mum had seen him yet. "What about meeting Mum and Ash and everyone?" I asked.

"I'm not sure it's on his mind right now. I get the feeling from Beth that he can't wait to leave and get back to London. Coming here hasn't worked out too well for him really has it? He came seeking answers and what did he get? An unwanted stay in hospital."

"When is he going?" I asked anxiously.

"Not sure, I think Beth was hoping it would be today or tomorrow."

"How is she?" I asked, genuinely interested.

"She's pretty pissed off with everything. She's quite tough, but I think she's found hanging around frustrating. She's away from home and she's been critical of his hospital care too. I don't know Dandie, she's not a bad person and I think under different circumstances you'd get on quite well with her."

I paused in thought for a few minutes.

"Charley, I think we should go and visit him," I declared.

"Oh, Dandie, I don't know if that's wise," Charley said, visibly shaken by the thought.

"Come on Charley, if we don't we'll be forever wondering. We have legitimate reasons for visiting him. He's conscious now and probably bored out of his mind. He'd love to see you, I'm sure it would be real surprise."

"Yep, it'd be a surprise alright!" Charley replied, unconvinced.

"Do you know what the visiting hours are?" I'd made up my mind, I had to meet Tom Bradley, I might never get another chance. I needed to tell Mum as well, just in case she wanted to see him, assuming she hadn't already visited him.

The thought just entered my head, maybe Mum had already been to see him. I stopped dead for a few seconds contemplating that thought.

"Charley, do you know if Sylvia has been to visit Tom in hospital?"

"Not that I know of," she replied. "I think Beth would have mentioned it if she had, wouldn't she?"

Charley texted Beth to check on the visiting times at the hospital. She texted back with the times: 2 – 4pm and 6 – 8pm. She didn't query why Charley had asked. Beth did add that they were hoping to take Tom home tomorrow, Sunday.

"Charley, I'm going whether you're coming or not, and I'm going to let Mum know too," I said decisively.
Charley sat quietly on the sofa, "I don't know Dandie, I'm not sure it's the right thing to do."
But my mind was made up. I phoned Dad and told him about Tom Bradley's plans. He told me that they hadn't been to the hospital to visit him and he wasn't sure Mum wanted to after all. He said he'd let me know and left it at that.

It was lunch time, I made brunch for Charley and me; a big fry-up of eggs, bacon, fried bread, fried tomatoes, fried mushrooms and baked beans on the side. Yeah, best hangover cure ever! Well it was a fighting start anyway, and I was only suffering a mild hangover to be fair.

The time passed surprisingly quickly. I didn't hear anything more from Dad, and Charley was beginning to come round to the idea of the hospital visit. I suspected she might join me. Although I'd decided to go, with or without her.

I needed to meet him, for all sorts of reasons. I'd seen the crash, I needed to know he was ok. Also, for curiosity's sake I really wanted to see what he looked like and what he was like as a person. I suppose a part of me almost wanted to vet him, just in case Mum did ever want to meet him. I needed to suss him out first, so we knew who we were dealing with.

Chapter twenty three

The visiting hour arrived much faster than I had anticipated. Although I was determined to go to the hospital, I had to admit to being slightly terrified. Seriously, think about it, this was a weird situation whichever way you looked at it. Going to hospital to visit a complete stranger, having witnessed his accident, and as an aside we also happened to be related without knowing it.

Charley and I arrived at the hospital, I didn't know what to bring, grapes, chocolates or flowers? In the end we opted for chocolate. Visiting hours had only just commenced, but we both knew that Beth would more than likely already be at Tom Bradley's bedside.

We walked onto the ward and approached the reception desk. Charley asked where we could find him and a very helpful nurse pointed us in the right direction. As we walked down the corridor towards his ward, I was thrown into panic.

"Charley, this is wrong, we can't do this. Come on let's leave," I said, tugging on Charley's skirt and turning around. She grabbed hold of my arm.
"No, Dandie, we're here now, we can't leave."
"We can Charley, he'll never know we've been. Please, I want to go," I pleaded. Charley held my arm tightly and gently steered me along the corridor. I felt extremely uncomfortable and couldn't think why I had ever thought it was a good idea.
"Dandie, we've come this far. He's just around the corner, and if we don't see him now we may never get another chance."

What Charley said made sense. She released the grasp of my arm. I stood still and took in a big deep breath.

"Ok, let's do this!" I said determinedly, pulling myself together.

We arrived at the ward, there were around eight beds in it. Some had curtains drawn around them. We stood frozen in the doorway.

"Which one is Tom Bradley?" we asked each other.

We slowly started to walk along the centre of the room. The beds were at right angles to the walls, evenly placed on both sides of the room with a central pathway in the middle. As we got about half way along the room Charley spotted Beth sitting next to a bed with a young dark haired man sitting upright in it. We both stopped in our tracks.

"Charley, hi! What are you doing here?" Beth called out when she spotted us standing in the middle of the room. We both tentatively walked closer to the bed.

"Um, we've brought chocolates," was all Charley could come up with for an answer. Tom looked up at us both.

"I know you," Tom said, looking at Charley. "We met in Venice, Charlotte, Charley isn't it? Well, what a surprise. What an earth are you doing here?" he seemed pleasantly taken aback.

"Hi Tom, heard about your accident. How are you?" she asked. Meanwhile Beth was looking perplexed.

"You know each other?" she asked, confused.

"Yeah, we met in Venice. Charley is the reporter I told you about," Tom replied, trying to sit up further in the bed. "How is it you are here, how did you know where to find me?"

Charley's appearance seemed to have completely blown his mind.

"Sorry Beth, let me introduce you. Beth this is Charley, Charley this is my girlfriend Beth" he said. "This is so bizarre!"

"We know each other Tom, Charley is my cousin, I've been staying with her all week," Beth explained. Then she turned accusingly to Charley, "Charley, why didn't you tell me you knew Tom?"

"I wasn't sure it was the same Tom," Charley replied, hesitantly.

"How come you came to visit him then?" Beth said becoming irritated.

"Dandie wanted to come and she wanted me to come with her," was the best Charley could come up with.

Suddenly Tom's expression changed and his interest turned directly to me. He looked at me in such a strange way. It was as though his eyes were looking into my soul. I realised then why Ash had said he looked familiar. Colouring aside, Tom Bradley looked like a smaller version of Ash. Same face shape, same eyes, even the same facial expressions. It was uncanny how alike they looked.

"What's your name?" he asked me, there was desperation in his tone of voice.

I hesitated, paused, took a deep breath and replied, "Dandie, Dandelion Jensen."

Tom, visibly stirred, tried to sit upright, almost trying to get out of the bed.

"Thank you," he said. I was confused; what was he thanking me for?

"Beth, please, get the girls some chairs," he said.

Beth went off to find a couple of chairs.

"Wow, this is a turn out," Tom said. "It's very nice to see you Charley, I was hoping to see you on my visit. Hadn't planned on it being like this though." Then he turned his attention to me.

"Dandelion, do you know who I am?" he asked me cautiously.

"I do now," I replied. "I saw your crash you know. It happened right outside my window. I saw you staggering when they pulled you out of the car, just before it burst into flames. You were very lucky. Totally screwed up my day by the way."

"Mine didn't go so well either," he replied. We all laughed nervously.

"Dandelion, I want you to know, I don't want to intrude in any way."

"You wanted to meet with Ash didn't you?" I asked.

"Yes, I thought he would be the easiest to contact. He never got back to me."

"He thought it was a wind up, didn't take it seriously."

"Oh," he replied, looking down at the bedclothes. Beth reappeared with a couple of chairs. Charley and I thanked her. Beth didn't look at all happy about our impromptu visit.

"Why didn't you tell me you were visiting?" she asked Charley.

"I didn't know I was until a couple of hours ago. Sorry Beth," Charley replied.

"Does it matter Beth?" Tom asked abruptly. Tom actually didn't seem that interested in Charley, he was much more focused on me. I felt embarrassed; I had no history with Tom, yet I was the one getting all the attention which didn't seem right somehow.

"Dandelion, I'm sorry we've met like this. I'd planned it all so differently." He hesitated before carrying on, "Please let me explain. My mother died last year; she was an amazing woman. She gave my sister Chloe and I such a wonderful life and we couldn't have wanted for anything better. Both my parents have always been entirely honest and up front with us. We have always known we were adopted." He paused, "Do you mind hearing this?" he asked me. I thought it was a bit strange, a complete stranger telling me his life story, but I was interested to hear what he knew.

"No, I don't mind," I replied, feeling uncomfortable and out of my depth, but there was a desperation about him. I wished Ash was there too.

"My sister Chloe knew quite a lot about her birth parents, she didn't have many unanswered questions. It seemed that because of that she never really had a big desire to dig deeper into her background." He paused again; he seemed to be in pain and getting tired.

"Are you ok?" Beth asked him. He reassured her that he was alright and continued.

"Dandelion, I knew nothing about my birth parents. My parents couldn't tell me a thing. They didn't know anything, but with their help, and a lot of detective work, we managed to get the name Sylvia Fisher, her date of birth, marriage certificate and details of her children."

"I think Mum wants to meet you," I interrupted. I felt awkward, like he was talking to the wrong person. It was Mum he should be talking to, not me, and not in a public place in front of Beth and Charley. As soon as I'd opened my mouth I regretted it. I only said it to stop him talking. I wasn't at all sure that she really did want to meet him and didn't want to get his hopes up. Tom got the hint and stopped talking.

"Does anyone want a cup of tea?" I offered and stood up. Everyone replied in the positive, I took my handbag and went in search of tea. Times like this make me wish I smoked, because it seemed like the perfect time to go outside for a fag. But I didn't smoke, so I had to make do with sitting in the corridor opposite the vending machine watching the tea pour out into the polystyrene cups. I thought about texting Ash and telling him where I was, but then I remembered how he had reacted when we talked about Tom before and thought better of it.

I thought about Mum, and Dad. Should I tell them where I was? I phoned Dad.
"Dad, hi. I'm at the hospital. I'm visiting Tom Bradley, thought you should know. It's all so weird, wish I hadn't come. It looks like he's going home tomorrow."
"You're very brave, Dandie. Thanks for letting me know. I'll tell Sylvie, but can't make any promises darling. This is tough for her, we can't underestimate how difficult bringing up the past is for her. I think she does want to meet him though, for his sake if nothing else."
"I know Dad, I'm sorry. He seems like a nice guy, if that counts for anything. He reminds me of Ash a little."
Funny that Dad thought I was brave, I didn't feel at all brave, quite the opposite. I sat for a few minutes in the hospital with four cups of tea beside me. I looked through some photos on my phone and came across some silly ones of the previous night with Ben. They made me smile. We'd been making faces and giggling at the camera.

I pulled myself together, took a deep breath and walked back to the ward carrying the cups on a tray.

Chapter twenty four

The three of them seemed to be getting along. Charley and Tom were reminiscing about Venice, Beth seemed interested and they were laughing. I was so relieved about that, jeez, that could have been awkward. I guess that the attraction was only on Charley's part then. I had to admit Beth and Tom did seem a tight couple.

When I joined them though, the atmosphere changed completely and took a more serious tone. I was sad about that. I felt like an intruder. I didn't know Tom Bradley at all, I was just a stranger caught up in a bizarre string of connections, none of which I had any control over. Beth and Charley both knew Tom well. It was an odd place to be; I wanted to leave. My curiosity had been satisfied; I had no more desire to be here.

"Hey, guys, I'm shooting off. Nice to have met you Tom, hope you feel better soon."
"No! Please, don't go!" Tom pleaded with me.
I felt embarrassed by his outburst.
"Umm, sorry, I've got things to do. You all have fun," I said feeling even more awkward.
"Please, Dandelion, stay. I've looked so hard for you, please stay just five minutes longer." He seemed so anguished. I stood frozen, looking around for some sort of escape. I really didn't know what to do.
"Charley, let's leave them alone for a while," Beth suggested, giving me a pleading look. Charley stood up and they both wandered off out of the ward, leaving me and Tom Bradley alone. I was still standing uncomfortably by the bed.
"Please, Dandelion, sit down," Tom said.

I sat down on the seat next to him.

"I really don't know what there is to say," I replied.

"Dandelion, I've been searching, with the help of my dad, for my birth mother for a long time."

I felt for him, really I did, but it was a mistake coming to the hospital without Mum and Dad.

"Umm, oh this is awkward. I don't know if there is a right or wrong way for people to meet in our situation, but this isn't what I had planned, I'm sorry," he paused, expectantly.

I really didn't know how to respond.

"Maybe I should have contacted Sylvia first?" he asked.

I couldn't think of a reply, so just shuffled my feet and looked at the ground. I wasn't handling this well at all.

"I got in contact with Ash initially, because I thought that we could meet, sort of like mates. I thought that would be a gentler way to meet the family, maybe that was wrong – anyhow, didn't exactly work out did it?" He seemed to be trying to excuse himself; I wanted to tell him there was no need, but felt locked in an uncomfortable silence.

He didn't continue. I think he was waiting for me to respond, but seriously, I didn't know what to say and I really just wanted to leave.

"Dandelion, how much do you know about me…and Sylvia?" he said cautiously.

I shrugged. "Until three days ago, nothing," I replied, finally finding my voice.

"Oh, I'm sorry," he replied. "I want you to know that I don't mean to intrude into your lives, at all. I'm just looking for some answers. Oh dear, this has turned out badly," he said apologetically.

"Look Tom, I'm really glad to have met you, but I've got to go, I'm sorry. Take care and I hope you feel better soon." I got up to leave and wished Charley and Beth would come back.

Tom looked at me; he seemed a little sad, but he smiled.

"Thanks for coming Dandie, I really appreciate it, really I do," he said, and then continued, "Maybe we'll see each other again?"

"Maybe," I replied, as I grabbed my bag and walked out of the ward, trembling.

Once in the corridor I literally ran towards the exit. I felt like such an idiot having gone there in the first place. Curiosity is not all it's cracked up to be you know, be aware. I had to ring Ash, I couldn't deal with this alone. I stood by the exit and got on my phone to him.

"Ash, please come to the hospital now, I really need you." Was the message I left on his voicemail. I didn't know if he would come with Ash there were never any certainties he was totally unpredictable.

My phone rang, *thank God Ash has rung,* I thought hopefully. It wasn't Ash, it was Ben.

"Hi Dandie, how are you feeling today?" he asked. I pulled myself together and replied.

"Fine, how about you?"

"You sound a bit odd, are you ok? Not hung-over are you? Sorry."

"No, not really, well just little bit," I tried to laugh and sound as normal as possible.

"I had a lovely evening," I said, feeling emotional.

"So did I, we should do it again sometime."

"Agreed," I replied smiling.

"Are you free today, tomorrow? When are you free?" he asked.

I was so tempted to say 'I'm free right now, pick me up and whisk me away' it would have been perfect. But I couldn't, it wouldn't be fair on anyone and I didn't want him to know about the craziness that was going on.

"I'm free tomorrow, anytime," I said, encouragingly.

"Ok, I'll tell you what, how about I pick you up around 2ish and take you out on a boat?"

"I'd love that Ben, thanks!" I said, excitedly.

"Done! I have the day off tomorrow so that will work out great, see you then," he said happily.

"Looking forward to it, thanks again Ben," I said, probably a bit too impassioned.

I let out a huge sigh, picked up my bag and walked out of the hospital, smiling. I pushed my worries to one side and focused on looking forward to a nice relaxing afternoon with Ben.

As I walked down the road on another glorious sunshiny day, I looked at the faces of people passing me by and wondered how their day had been so far. I genuinely hoped that they were having a nice day. In reality though, chances aren't that great if they're wandering around outside a hospital.

I wanted to get away as far as I could from the hospital and headed towards town. My phone rang again, this time it was Ash.

Relieved, I answered.

"Hi Ash," I said.

"Dandie, are you ok. You're in hospital, what's happened, have you been in an accident? I'm on my way right now, are you in A&E?"

129

"Whoa, Ash slow down, jeez! I'm fine, nothing's happened to me."

"Phew, seriously Dandie, you scared the life out of me! Leaving me messages about being in hospital! What the hell?"

"Oh, Ash I'm sorry, really I am. I went there to visit Tom, Tom Bradley, you know the guy in the crash. It was such a mistake!"

"What the...why?" Ash said, sounding increasingly confused.

"Ash, he's looking for answers. I didn't know what to say, it felt so awkward. I should never have gone."

"Are you there now Dandie?" Ash asked down the phone, quite calmly I thought considering this was Ash.

"No, I had to leave, I'm heading into town."

"Does Mum know?" he asked. I said I wasn't sure.

"Time I visited Tom Bradley," Ash said, and hung up the phone.

"Why?" I asked, but he'd already hung up.

Great! I thought. *OK, looks like I'm heading back.* I turned around and retraced my steps back to the hospital. I had to be there with Ash, as there was no knowing what he might do.

Chapter twenty five

As I approached the hospital again, my heart felt heavy. I really didn't want to return, but at the same time I felt some sort of strange responsibility; I'd called Ash and started this off. I dragged my feet and almost wished for a distraction. I thought the best plan of action was to hang outside the building and wait for him to turn up. Tom Bradley wasn't out to upset us, he was just looking for answers, which was his right. I felt for him, really I did, but, at the same time, he wasn't our responsibility. This was his journey of discovery.

Ash, on the other hand, seemed to have gone into full on over-protective mode, completely unnecessarily if you asked me. Seriously he was acting like a complete asshole.

Ash drove into the car park, driving far too fast. I walked up to the car, not really knowing what to expect.

"Hi," I said, testing.

"Dandie," he replied, abruptly.

"Ash, just take a minute," I said.

"Dandie, I'm fine. Let's just get this over with shall we. See what this trouble maker wants."

"Ash, he's not a trouble maker, he's just looking for answers, that's all. Chill!"

"Hey little sis', I'm not going to make a 'scene', but this needs sorting out. If Tom Bradley wants to meet us then let's get it over with."

There was nothing more I could do, so with an *omg here we go* fatalistic feeling, I reluctantly led Ash to Tom's bed.

Tom Bradley startled when he saw Ash enter the ward. Beth and Charley were at his side. All eyes turned to Ash. He was not going to offer any compassion that was clear. I felt nervous, Ash could be volatile. Seriously, what was his problem?

Ash walked straight up to Tom Bradley's bedside. Beth held Tom's hand, Charley backed away and I stood behind Ash, nervously. I quickly intervened,
"Ash, meet Tom Bradley. Tom this is Ash Jensen," and stepped back.

"Dandie, you came back! I'm so pleased, and you brought Ash? Ash I'm so pleased to meet you. Thank you for coming. I'm sorry I'm stuck in this bed like this, it really isn't how I thought things would be," Tom offered.

There was a moment of silence that was excruciating and seemed to last forever. No one really knew what to say or do. I was surprised at Ash's reaction. He'd seemed so aggressive initially, now though he just seemed a bit gobsmacked.

Surprisingly, Ash walked up to Tom's bedside and reached out his hand to him and shook it. I gave out a huge sigh of relief. I don't know what Ash was afraid of, but whatever it was, it seemed to have subsided, much to my relief!

"You don't look so great," Ash said.
Tom smiled. "No, not feeling my best," he replied. "Look, I didn't mean any harm, mate, I was just looking for some answers. Maybe I could have handled it better?"

I jumped in, "Tom, really, there's no need. It's all been a bit of a shock for everyone, we didn't know anything about you."
"Yeah, I kind of sussed that, sorry," Tom replied.

"When you contacted me I thought it was a windup," Ash said.

"No windup, I'm for real, I'm afraid," Tom replied. "You knew nothing of me?"

Silence followed as we all felt, and probably looked, awkward. Beth and Charley both watched anxiously.

"Not until a few days ago…" I said, instantly regretting that I'd opened my mouth; it was just that I couldn't stand the silence, so I had to say something.

"Sorry," Tom replied.

"Why didn't you contact Mum?" I quickly asked.

Tom paused before answering.

"I don't know… I thought about it, but then I hatched a plan that if I met with Ash, on a man-to-man level, hopefully we could become mates and I could gently introduce my true identity. I suppose it was a bit sneaky of me… and cowardly. Either way, it didn't exactly pan out did it?"

"Unconventional way of doing things," I replied thoughtfully.

"You'll fit right well with our family," Ash said

Just then Charley stood bolt upright.

"Hello Sylvie, Jim!" Charley said loudly.

We all turned around, Mum and Dad were standing behind us. Mum looked absolutely terrified, and Dad was holding onto her tightly and reassuringly.

"Hello Charley," Mum said quietly and smiled at her.

Charley whispered in Beth's ear and they both quietly stood up leaving Ash, Mum, Dad and myself alone with Tom.

"Tom Bradley, I presume? Nice to meet you, I'm Jim and this is my wife Sylvie," Dad said giving Tom a firm handshake.

Tom looked taken aback, but also elated.
It felt so uncomfortable, for everyone. I didn't know where to look, what to say or do. I turned to Ash for reassurance, but he looked as awkward as I did. So we just stood there frozen to the spot like a pair of lemons.

Tom's gaze was firmly fixed on Mum. His facial expression was something to behold. I can't quite describe it. He had a look of longing, despair even, but he also looked happy and intrigued, like he was expecting for something extraordinary to happen. Indeed this whole set up was extraordinary.

To my surprise Mum was struck dumb. She didn't utter a word. She too seemed frozen to the spot and was also staring at Tom, but her look was one of surprise and shock. Dad, typical Dad, intervened and took control of the situation.

"Tom, welcome to our family. Well done for tracking us down, we're very pleased to meet you. First things first though, how are you? You look like you've been pretty badly knocked about. What actually happened?" Thank you Dad! He could always be relied on to take command of any given situation and defuse it if necessary. Somehow he had this knack of making everything seem normal and acceptable. He was always completely non-judgemental and fair, always open to listening.

"Hello Mr Jensen, sir. I was in a pretty bad crash, I really don't remember much about the accident, I just remember that I was excited about my trip here. I had a few meetings planned and the day was to be a bit of an exciting adventure really; the adventure wasn't quite the one I had in mind though. I badly damaged my knees, but I'll be ok. I think I'm going to be discharged tomorrow, hopefully. The last few days have been a bit of a blur, I'll be glad to leave and get home to be honest."

"Please, Tom, don't call me sir. Jim will do just fine," Dad replied. "I'm really sorry to hear of your accident, that's very bad luck."

Dad turned to look at Mum, standing quietly next to him. She suddenly appeared to be so small and vulnerable. I reconnected with my muscles and walked towards her. I stood next to her and held her tight as I could feel her body trembling. I looked at Dad.

Tom tried desperately to sit up further in his bed, looking pained as he did.
Mum squeaked, "I'm so terribly terribly sorry."
"Mrs Jensen, can I call you Sylvia?" Tom asked. She didn't reply, just nodded, "You don't need to apologise for anything."

Mum walked slowly towards Tom. She sat herself down on the chair next to his bed. I watched and waited silently not knowing what was to follow.

"You are beautiful," she said to him. "Are you happy?"
"Yes," he replied. "I'm very happy."
Mum visibly let out a sigh of relief. "I'm so pleased, I didn't know, I worried so much about you."
"No need to have worried Sylvia. My parents were lovely and I couldn't have wanted for anything better, really," he

said reassuringly. I have to admit to being very impressed with Tom Bradley, he was handling the situation much better than any of us.

"I want you to know, my quest was purely one of curiosity. My mother died recently and, with the help of my father I tracked you down. I have often wondered about you. Chloe, my sister, knew much more about her background than I did about mine, so I suppose I felt I ought to find out more. I'm very sorry if I've caused distress."
"Oh really Tom, please don't apologise, you have nothing at all to apologise for. I'm the one who should be apologising, I'm the one who abandoned you." She paused, "I'm so glad you found me. To hear that you've had a happy life means more to me than I can put into words."

Mum looked up at Dad for reassurance. He winked at her.
"He looks like Ash," she said to dad, as if no one else was listening. He nodded but didn't say anything, he just put his hand on her shoulder reassuringly. Mum then looked apologetically at me and Ash. "I'm sorry," she said to us.

"Sylvie, stop apologising to everyone, no one's cross with you," Dad said, giving her a strong hug and kissing her on the cheek.

"It means so much to me that I'm here next to you, Tom said to Mum and held out his hand to her. Apprehensively she took it. As they touched it was as though a spark of electricity passed between them, and they both slightly jumped.
"Ash, how about getting everyone some tea?" said Dad. Ash agreed and slunk off to the tea machine, probably relieved to have escaped the situation.

"Would you mind if I asked 'Why?'" Tom said nervously to Mum.

She looked up at Dad, who held her firmly and nodded.

Mum took a very deep breath, sighed and coughed. I thought she was about to be sick. She regained her composure and began.

"Oh my, this is the hardest thing I have ever had to say... please understand I had no choice." She paused looking directly at Tom, he patiently waited for her to continue.

"I was fifteen, a young woman, a child really," she tried hard to remain composed and it was visibly obvious she was struggling. "I had no choice but to let you go."

"That is what I'd suspected," Tom said quickly. I think he was trying to ease my Mum.

"It was all taken out of my control," she continued.

"I understand," he said. "You were young, too young for the responsibly and you probably didn't have the support?"

It was as though Tom Bradley had thought it all out already.

Mum paused, she looked again at Dad for reassurance and then directed her gaze at me. I felt that she was questioning whether she should continue or not.

"Please Tom, let me tell you," Mum continued, visibly choked. "I was young, and silly. Very naïve and thoughtless. I... I thought that if I ignored everything, the pregnancy ... it would all go away. I'm so very sorry."

Tom listened silently to what she had to say.

Mum hesitated and again glanced at dad for support, he blew her a kiss and smiled. I walked over and stood by her.

"You probably have questions about your biological father?" she looked at Tom, he nodded quietly.

"I'm so sorry to say, I... I can't really tell you anything. He was a stranger, a 'one night stand'. He never knew about you, nobody did." Mum had turned her gaze to the ground and a tear fell from her cheek. She shrugged and pulled herself together.

"Tom, what I did was terrible and I regretted the whole episode more than I can say, please forgive me."

Tom looked directly at her.

"There's nothing to forgive. You gave me life for which I am eternally grateful, thank you."

Wow! I thought to myself. I felt it was time to leave them alone together and went off to find Ash.

Chapter twenty six

The past few days had been extraordinary, that's for sure. Was there some weird planetary alignment spooking up the atmosphere or whatever it supposedly does? Seriously, my life wasn't usually so eventful. 'Things' just don't happen to me. I'm quite happy with my life being predictable and, dare I say it, boring. Running out of coffee first thing in the morning is more than enough excitement for me.

Ash on the other hand has always been an adrenaline junkie, but I think even these events have tested him. I thought of Rose, what she would do if she were here, I really didn't know but felt pretty sure it wouldn't be anything helpful.

I found Ash and sat with him at the drinks machine. I turned my thoughts to my date with Ben tomorrow on the river. I was really looking forward to that. How relaxing it was going to be gently floating along and really slowing down the pace, chilling with Ben.

Thinking of Ben brought a smile to my face, he was really cool. He wasn't demanding, he was really easy to be with, and fun too. He made me laugh; it wasn't so much what he said, more how he said and did things which made me laugh. He seemed uncomplicated. I wondered what future I'd have with him and giggled to myself.

"Why are you laughing Dandie?" Ash asked, confused.
"Oh, I don't know Ash, just thinking about stuff," I replied, not really paying attention to the question.

I haven't spent much time in hospitals, luckily. They are pretty depressing places to be in. No wonder Tom was keen to leave. There's a kind of uniform blue-grey in the overall colour. You can tell they've tried to brighten the place up with colourful curtains and furnishings, but there's no getting away from the utilitarian colour scheme. There are long wide corridors with nursing staff constantly walking up and down pushing trollies or wheel chairs. Frail people, old and young cautiously make their way along the corridors, from where and to who knows, I guess the most depressing thing about hospitals, is that whichever way you look at it, people are there because something is wrong with their health.

"Ash, tell me something to cheer me up, please," I said.
"Hmm, let me think," he replied. "No, I've got nothing."
"I have this crazy 'friend' at work Ash. She's called Jade. She's getting married to the poor Mike. It's all very sweet and everything, but I just can't help feeling a little bit sorry for Mike. I get the impression that he doesn't really get a say in many things."
"Maybe that suits him," Ash replied, rather bluntly I thought.
"Yeah, maybe, but you'd think he'd want some input into the decision making wouldn't you?"
"Dunno, sounds like he's opted for the easy life. From mother to wife, never having to organise anything, just being looked after for ever more. Jeez Dandie, that's depressing, thought you wanted cheering up?"

"Oh Ash, I just don't know what to do. This whole situation, it's just mind blowing. I wish she'd told us before. It would have been so much easier to deal with. Why did they think it was a good idea to hide it from us? I mean, jeez, it's not like it's a tea cup or something, Tom is a whole human being; how can you hide a whole human being from a family? I know it was tough on Mum, but really, shouldn't we have been told, it must have dawned on them that he'd eventually seek Mum out?" I was confused, and frankly disappointed. I felt betrayed by my own mother.

"Yeah, maybe, but Dandie, this isn't about you, me or Rose, it's about Mum. I'm sure she did what she thought was best for us, misguided maybe, but you know damn well that Mum would never do anything to intentionally upset anyone."

Wow, wise words coming from Ash, this was a first. Maybe he had a sensitive soul after all, hidden underneath all that bravado. I was impressed.
"Maybe we should go back and check on Mum and Dad?" I suggested.
"Agreed," replied Ash, with that we both got up and carrying the tray of polystyrene cups of tea, made our way back to the dorm where Tom Bradley was holed up.

Ash and I walked slowly along the grey-blue corridor of the hospital ward. A trolley came towards us being pushed by a strong, young, male nurse. All of a sudden a squeal came from the trolley.
"Ash! Ash, what are you doing here?" came a female voice from the trolley.
Here we go! I thought to myself as we approached her.
"Em, what are you doing here, like this?" Ash said, bending over the trolley to hug the girl.
"Oh nothing much, off to have an x-ray. I fell off my bike and think I've broken my leg. Looks worse than it is I'm sure." She was visibly in a huge amount of pain but still managed to giggle flirtingly at Ash. Seriously, this sort of

141

thing could only happen to Ash, patient in agony coming on to able-bodied visitor.

He bent over her trolley and gave her a kiss. "Ring me when you're out of here," he said to her.

"You bet," replied Em, beaming.

As we continued on our separate ways, I gave Ash a 'look'.

"What?" he protested.

"Who was she?" I asked.

"Em," Ash replied, as though that was all the information that was required.

I simply shrugged, I had more important things on my mind. I do find it extraordinary though, how Ash could find romance literally anywhere. How did he do it? I guess he got my share of magnetic personality, shame.

As we approached Tom Bradley's ward, I became overcome with a sense of unease and nervous anticipation. Part of me was in a hurry to check that everyone was ok, I was excited to see what developments there had been, but there was also a part of me that felt we were almost intruding on a very personal situation. When we got to the room, however, I was surprised to find Tom and Beth alone with no sign of Mum, Dad or Charley.

"Hi, where's Mum and Dad?" I asked, putting the tray down on the side table.

"They've gone," Tom replied. He seemed tired and thoughtful. He and Beth were holding hands and smiling, looking relaxed and content. I could sense a lot of tenderness and caring between them.

Ok, this was awkward. What had just happened, surely Ash and I had only been gone for a few minutes? Beth and Tom looked at us expectantly and I didn't know what to do. I decided it was probably best to leave and tugged at Ash's arm.

"Tom, Beth, Ash and I are going to go now. It was lovely to meet you, really it was. I do hope you get better soon," I said to him, and turned to leave. Ash was hesitant though, he still had unfinished business with Tom. "Ash, we're leaving. Walk away, please," I said quietly to Ash. He was reticent I could tell.

"You don't need to go," Tom said quickly.

I stood dead in my tracks, not really knowing what to do. I wasn't ready to become all pally with Tom just yet. I needed more time to digest everything and desperately wanted to leave. Ash on the other hand was like 'Ivan the Inquisitor', eager to sit down and question him.

"I'm staying," stated Ash, as he pulled up a chair and made himself comfortable, "I want to get to know you dude," he said smiling at Tom.

Lordy lordy, I thought to myself. Whatever! Ash could stay and get all matey with Tom, I needed a break so said my goodbyes and left them to it.

As I reluctantly left Ash in the company of our new found family member, my thoughts went back to Mum. I was surprised, and confused, that she had left so quickly. Had something happened? I was very concerned about her. I couldn't stop wondering why she had kept such a huge secret from us for all these years. It seemed so out of character. I wanted to go and see her.

A week ago, we were an ordinary happy family with nothing major to worry about. Then Tuesday happened and I realised our lives would never be the same again. It's amazing what a difference a day can make. You know, one can wander through days, weeks, even years, with everything being pretty much steady. Then boom, one day and a series of bizarre events, everything is turned upside down. Incredible.

Chapter twenty seven

I thought the best course of action was to go back to my flat. As I wearily made my way up the stairs to my front door I wondered what had happened between Tom Bradley and Mum. I couldn't even begin to imagine the emotions that must have surfaced during their encounter. I wondered if it was what Tom had been hoping for. A little part of me hoped so, and that he could now return to his life in peace. What about Mum? How must she be feeling, for her this was pretty unexpected. Had it been a relief or a nightmare?

On my doorstep was a posy of wild flowers. What a surprise, I'd never had flowers left for me before, ever! Who could they be from, nobody leaves flowers on doorsteps, do they? There was no note or any kind of clue as to where they had come from. They were tied together with a piece of fine string. Beginning to wilt, I picked them up and sniffed them, they smelt sweet. I unlocked my door and went straight to the kitchen and filled a glass with water and put the flowers in. I smiled. What a lovely gesture, I didn't mind who they were from, someone cared enough to think of me and go to the trouble of somehow getting into my hallway and laying them on the doorstep. I felt very happy about that. Could it have been Ben, would he do something like that? More likely to be a girl, Charley maybe, knowing how tricky things were and trying to cheer me up? All I can say that it worked, I really did feel happier than I did five minutes ago.

I made a cup of coffee and sat down at the table. I pulled out all the information I'd gathered about Venice; how magical it all looked. I had such a strong desire to get away and travel. I had no ties, I was young and I had money! I thought of Ben, wondered if he would, or could come with me. Crazy I know seeing as how I didn't really know him, but he struck me as someone who would be a good travelling companion.

You know what, enough procrastinating, I was going to book a holiday and I was going to do it right then! I can't remember the last time I went abroad. I went onto the internet, found some cheap flights and booked a return flight for one, for seven days in Venice, result! How was that for spontaneity? I felt excited, but at the same time slightly terrified. I had now committed myself to a week on my own in a foreign country where I didn't speak the language. It would be fine, I reassured myself. I'd have a wonderful time and was bound to meet people and make new friends, now for a hotel to stay in. It was fun trawling through all the different hotel sites, to be fair they all seemed pretty amazing to me. Looking at all the pictures really whet my appetite for travel.

I found a reasonably priced hotel near to the Teatro La Fenice. My plan of escapism was coming together nicely, I was determined to make something good and positive out of today. It had been my dream to visit Venice for as long as I could remember so I felt very pleased with myself. See you really can make dreams come true, it's all a state of mind. If an opportunity presents itself to you, grab it and make the most of it.

I had to text Charley and tell her, she could give me tips and advice on what to do and see there, she might even want to join me?

The doorbell rang and I wondered who it could be? I went to the buzzer, it was my good friend Jacinta. I let her in.

"Hello darling, long time no see! How are you?" we both exclaimed, having not seen each other for a few weeks.

"Oh, Dandie, I've been meaning to pop round for ages, what news?"

"Well, I've only gone and booked myself a week in Venice!" I exclaimed excitedly.

"Wow! When are you going, that's going to be amazing?" she asked.

"I know, I'm flying out at the end of the month. Bit of a spontaneous decision, but it's been a pretty unusual week all things considered."

"You lucky thing, I've never been to Venice but have heard it's wonderful. On another note, do you have plans for tonight, Dandie? I'm meeting up with some friends in town and we're going on to a club, come with us it'll be fun."

"Hey Jacinta, that sounds great. Definitely up for a good night out, yay!" Jacinta's timing was perfect.

We opened a bottle of vodka, chatted about outfits and danced around my living room to the music on my sound system. It had been a while since I had been on a girl's night out so I was looking forward to it and I knew it was going to be a laugh.

Jacinta was great fun, larger than life with a big personality; loud, outgoing and always up for a good time, she was just the tonic I needed. I couldn't have planned it better.

After a few hours of drinking vodka and getting dressed up, we were ready to hit the town. We literally danced our way along the pavements towards the town centre. It was very dark, but the street lights were so bright you could be forgiven for thinking it was daytime. Big groups of people were gathering in town, laughing, shouting and generally having a good time.

We made it to the bar where Jacinta had arranged to meet some friends. The place was heaving, the music and laugher very loud. We squeezed our way around until we found her friends. A couple of them I already knew and it was good to catch up again.

There was some cool nineties indie music playing and the atmosphere was buzzing. The bar consisted of two large rooms with high ceilings, painted deep red. Out the back was a large conservatory leading to a smoker's courtyard. It was so refreshing to be there. What a difference a change of scene can make. All the confusion and thoughts of the last few days just evaporated into the heady mix of alcohol and body sweat. I felt like a great weight had been lifted from my shoulders; onwards and upwards Dandelion, time to party.

I've known Jacinta for years, we'd been school buddies. I've always been the quieter one, and she has always dipped in and out of my life, as she did with so many people. She has a wide and varied network of friends and a big heart. She was dependable for a good night out, and liked to party hard. A night out with Jacinta would never be quiet. She was just the tonic I needed right now, cheers!

The Retreat was a fun place to be. I looked around at all the faces, male, female, young and not so young, but mostly all were laughing and having a good time. There was a cool vibe in there, and that magical feeling that anything could happen and anything was possible.

Jacinta was never short of male attention, and it became a source of entertainment for us all. Molly, Vicky, Anna and myself would 'bet' on which unsuspecting male would make a move on Jacinta next. The thing about Jacinta is that she's a dreadful tease. I don't know how she gets away with it. She will flirt outrageously with a man, but very rarely does it go any further. It's like a game for her, and funny to witness. Like bees to honey they are drawn to her, she'll share a laugh or a dance, but they'll not be any physical contact, not even a kiss. I can't work out if she really loves men and craves the attention, or if she hates men and likes to wind them up. Either way she gets away with it and perhaps because no promises or physical exchanges are made, everyone seems happy.

After a couple of hours in the bar, we left and headed into the dizzy lights of town on a Saturday night. We all linked arms and sang our way along the streets, heels clicking on the pavement. It was a clear night and the sky was filled with pretty white stars shining brightly against the backdrop of the black night sky. For a few moments life felt free and uncluttered.

We arrived at a club and joined the queue of punters waiting to go in. Two big burly bouncers stood in front of the door like medieval guards protecting the entrance to a walled settlement. I could almost visualise them wearing a barbute and plackart, holding their pikes at the ready.

We didn't have to wait long before being invited inside, which was a good thing as it was getting a bit chilly hanging around outside at midnight. Inside the club the music was pounding so loudly it was impossible to hear anything anyone tried to say. We hit the dancefloor immediately, any thoughts of feeling cold disappeared in an instant. It felt good to dance, being lost in the music, feeling the rhythm flow through my body. I decided dance was excellent for the body and mind; I really should do it more often.

Anna went to the bar and bought a round of drinks as we stepped to the side of the dance floor and found a bench to sit down on. The club had some really wacky lighting, each wall seemed to have a different colour of light on it, so one wall would look blue, another red, purple, yellow and so on. The dancefloor was lit from beneath in a similar colour scheme, it was all a bit retro and I wasn't convinced it worked really. It seemed a bit disjointed somehow. Anyhow, the music was good and the drinks were not extortionate, so there wasn't really anything to complain about.

Suddenly Vicky shrieked, "Look it's Josh Kane!"
"Noo way," Molly said in her deep husky voice, "Where?"
"Look, over there, I'm sure that's him."
Everyone's eyes followed Vicky's gaze. Josh Kane, the hottest film star of the moment, what on earth would he be doing in this low budget club? I wasn't convinced it was him. Jacinta stood up to get a better view.
"It is him, Vicky!" she said excitedly.

Suddenly the evening had taken on a whole new dimension. People like Josh Kane didn't come to our town, ever.
"Is there some filming going on locally?" Anna asked. It would seem a logical explanation. It didn't appear as though he'd drawn much attention, yet. "We should invite him over, he looks lonely," she suggested jokingly.
"Ok," replied Jacinta.
"Noo," we all replied in unison, but it was too late. Jacinta was off to do what Jacinta did best. We watched her, slightly in awe, as she approached him and inevitably struck up a conversation. He was with a couple of other guys, but they were keeping a respectful distance, body guards perhaps? Do film stars really have them?

Whatever, Josh seemed to be happily engaged in Jacinta's charm offensive.

Josh Kane, in case you don't know, is a twenty-something English actor whose attractiveness and sex appeal is literally off the scale. Hot is an understatement. He had a string of box office hits, playing odd-ball characters. He is a brilliant actor and, according to the hype, a genuinely nice guy. What his relationship status was, I had no idea. What he was doing in this town in the back of beyond was even more of a mystery, maybe he was lost?

"No she isn't!" exclaimed Anna, in shock.
"Yes she is!" confirmed Molly.
We all looked on, dumbstruck, as we watched Jacinta walk towards us, with Josh Kane in tow!

"Josh, meet my friends: Molly, Dandie, Anna and Vicky," she said by way of an introduction.
"Hi," we all nervously replied, spontaneously acting like a gaggle of teenage school girls.
"May I join you?" he asked politely.
No one answered, but we all nervously moved up to make some space for him to sit down. My heart had leapt into my throat and I had become incapable of speech. Was this really happening?

"So, Josh, how come you're here in our town?" Vicky asked.
"Escaping," he replied. I couldn't believe he actually spoke, I needed someone to pinch me to make sure I wasn't dreaming.
"Escaping?" Molly repeated.
"Yeah, sometimes you just need to get away from it all, don't you?" he replied.

"Oh yes!" I piped up, and then instantly put my hand over my mouth, as if to shut myself up.

"But why here?" Vicky asked again.

Josh turned to look at Vicky, it was as if he needed to study her face and think very carefully about his answer.

"You know, I was just driving along the motorway and feeling really fed up so I took the next exit. What the hell, I thought, never been here before, never even heard of this place. How refreshing is that? An impromptu mystery tour, just the ticket. It's a nice little town you have here, very pretty and olde worlde. I was surprised it had so much going on."

How could it be that we were sitting in a nightclub chatting to an A-list celebrity? Now don't get me wrong, I'm not some celebrity-obsessed freak, in fact I'm more the opposite and have little interest in the lives of the rich and famous; they are not my friends, they don't have an impact on my life and frankly I've got more interesting things to think about. However, sitting in close proximity to a real live super star was just a teeny bit awe inspiring, even I had to admit. Plus, he was gorgeous!

Josh was very generous and bought us all several rounds of drinks, it was a little embarrassing and overwhelming, but I for one wasn't going to turn an offer of a drink down. Jacinta asked Josh to dance and they took to the dancefloor. He was good fun and great company, very easy going and relaxed. Watching them both on the dance floor reminded me of the dance scene in Pulp Fiction with John Travolta and Uma Thurman, it was very cool indeed.

Jacinta was tall and willowy, with brown very straight mid-length hair. She always wore bright red lipstick and false eyelashes. She was immaculately dressed in a classic style,

152

smart and smooth. She cut a striking vision. We always teased her about her name because she didn't like it to be shortened. It seemed obvious to call her Jac, but she hated it and would go off in a rage if she was called anything other than the full version of Jacinta. This inevitably made her a perfect target for winding up; it was just too simple, all we had to do was call her Jac!

I got the impression that Josh really enjoyed our company. Strangely he didn't attract much other attention; maybe people didn't recognise him or weren't interested, I don't know, but he seemed very relaxed with us and he was fun company. We quickly got over the 'superstar' intimidation and treated him just like a regular guy, almost. There was no agenda either, it was simply friendly. I think he really appreciated our company and at the end of the evening he paid for a taxi to take us home. What a gent!

Chapter twenty eight

It was 4.30am when I got home, what a great night that had turned out to be. Isn't it often the way that the best times are the ones that are spontaneous and unplanned? Meeting and spending time with Josh Kane was enlightening and memorable. It's odd, but because it seemed so understated and intimate, I didn't feel like rushing out and telling anyone about it. Somehow that would have felt like an act of betrayal.

I needed to get some sleep as I had a hot date to look forward to. I fell into the snug and cosy comfort of my bed and a deep restful sleep.

I woke up at midday, sunlight beamed through a gap in my bedroom curtains onto my bed. It took a few seconds for me to work out what day it was. My head felt decidedly foggy on this bright day. I turned on my mobile, there was a text from Ben. He wanted me to meet him at the boating station and asked if I could bring a bottle of wine. I really didn't fancy any wine, would it be cool to take juice instead, but then he was probably looking forward to a bottle of wine. I'd take both, problem solved. I texted him back to say I would be there in an hour and apologised for my tardiness.

Everything was cool. Yesterday was just another day which had passed, albeit leaving an interesting legacy, but hey, I had a hot date with Ben to focus on. Quick shower and browse through the wardrobe and I was back on track. Head wasn't as bruised as it should have been, but I wasn't complaining about that!

I couldn't help thinking about Mum though. All these distractions had been very welcome and certainly served a purpose, but I really was worried about mum. I found comfort in the fact that I knew she had Dad to look after and support her. A part of me did think they should be left alone right now to mull over things, but I wanted reassurance I guess that she was ok. Was that selfish? This did put me in a bit of a quandary, on the one hand I was really looking forward to a chilled out day with Ben and the possibility of something more; but also I had Mum's situation niggling in my head too.

You know what? I thought, *I'm not up to multi-tasking right now. I'll just go with the flow and head off to see Ben.* I would catch up with Mum later. Tom Bradley should have been leaving today, if he hadn't already, I didn't know if I would see him again.

It was another beautiful day, getting out into the fresh air did me the world of good. I took in a deep breath and spontaneously smiled. I had a good feeling about today and was surprised at how much I was looking forward to seeing Ben. All the weird stuff that had happened over the past few days were completely unconnected to Ben and he had become my escape from confusion and mixed-up emotions. Spending the afternoon with him felt like entering into a parallel universe. I grabbed a bottle of wine and a carton of juice from a shop on the way, and finally reached the boathouse. There Ben was waiting patiently.
"How do?" he greeted with that gorgeous sexy smile. I did momentarily think, *Ben could get any girl he wanted to with that smile, why me?* But it was only a momentary thought, because I reckon I deserved a bit of ego massaging, I'd been neglected for far too long.

"I brought wine," I said, cheerily holding up the bottle as proof.

"Great, I brought a picnic!" Ben replied, holding up a basket in return. For a split second I just stood there, beaming, looking at him and thinking how very lucky I felt. I almost wanted to pause time and just soak it up a bit longer.

"Your boat awaits you, ma'am," Ben offered, gesturing towards the elegant wooden rowing boat. I walked towards it and he held out his hand to help me aboard. I felt like royalty. He placed the wicker picnic basket at the end of the boat and in he climbed. In my slightly foggy head state, I almost felt like I was dreaming as it was such a surreal experience. *Who needs drugs,* I thought, *when reality is so awesome!*

Ben pushed the boat away from the bank and gently rowed down river. It was so peaceful and still. Sure there were other people out on their boats, and ducks and swans and other wildlife joining in the fun, but to me right at that moment it felt as though Ben and I and the boat were the only things on the river. I lay back, relaxed, with the heat of the sun on my face.

We rowed down river for about forty minutes away from the town and out in the open countryside. The fields were flat and quiet, and along the river bank reeds stood tall erect and still, there was hardly any breeze. Along the river's edge were clumps of water lilies, their whitish-pink bulbous flowers opening up to welcome the sun's rays. The sky was blue and still; there was the odd white cloud, but they hardly moved at all. Most of the boats didn't come this far, so apart from the odd one or two we were alone. Ben obviously knew his way around the river very well; how lucky was I to be there with him?

"We'll stop for lunch just up here," Ben said as we approached a sand bank. It resembled a small beach. Golden yellow sand, though more muddy than sea sand, sloped gently up the side of the river bank where it intermingled with grass trying to reclaim its position. Ben got out of the boat, his long slender legs striding the water between the boat and the sand bank. He pulled the boat up onto the beach and reached out his hand to help me climb out. I could easily have got out without any help, but it was nice that he offered. As I stood up, I fell slightly towards him and our bodies momentarily touched. There was a second or two of hesitation and then we both stood back.

Ben reached down into the boat and pulled out the picnic basket and a red-checked blanket, which he laid out on top of the grassy bank. I was being well and truly spoilt, and if the truth be known, seduced. We both sat down on the large, red blanket which felt soft to touch. I watched him as he started to unpack the basket. His dark wavy hair just touched the bottom of his neck and he had a fringe of wavy curls. His eyes were large and dark brown and his complexion was olive. His face was very angular and he reminded me a little of a Burne-Jones painting. He had a kind and smiley face.

I helped him unpack the basket, "Wow, Ben, you've got everything in here! Baguettes, dips, crisps, strawberries and cream, cucumber sandwiches, kebabs, scotch eggs, wow!"
"Haha, I didn't know what you like, so I just grabbed everything I could from the supermarket," he laughed. He really did get everything, perhaps an odd mix of things, but

what a feast. I felt like a cheapskate with my bottle of budget wine and carton of juice as my total contribution.

I opened the bottle of wine and poured out two glasses; Ben had brought along wine glasses too! Previous thoughts of abstinence had vanished from my consciousness.

Chapter twenty nine

We lay on the red-checked blanket, eating, drinking, teasing and laughing for a long time. I was so happy to be right there, right then. I couldn't think of anywhere I'd rather be. "I'm having such a great time, cheers Ben," I said, holding up my wine glass to him. He smiled, leaned towards me and we clinked glasses. Then he leaned a bit closer towards me, our lips met and we kissed. I fell gently backwards as he embraced me. We made love on the blanket on the river bank, hidden by the tall grass.

I lay on my back, eyes closed, feeling the heat of the sun's rays on my face and exposed skin. Ben lay beside me, arms wrapped around my body. I could happily have lain like that for hours, it felt so perfect and blissful. A cheeky duck approached what was left of our food and began pecking at it. Ben quickly jumped up and shooed the duck, and its friends who'd come to join in the free for all, back onto the river. As he returned, he picked some wild flowers which were growing on the bank and handed them to me.

"Was it you who left the bunch of flowers outside my door?" I asked.
"Busted!" Ben replied laughing.
"But, how did you get in the building?" I asked, genuinely curious.
"I can't tell you all my secrets!" he replied teasingly. Hmm, I thought, Ben's quite the romantic. This was new territory for me and I liked it, very much.
"This has been a really lovely day," I said.
"You sound surprised!" Ben replied.
"Well not surprised exactly, just unexpected."

"Haha, which bit was unexpected and which bit was not a surprise?" Ben replied.

"Oh, now you're messing with me! I was not surprised it would be a nice day, but the way it turned out was unexpected – in a very nice way." I smiled and leaned over to kiss him.

"We could do it again?" Ben suggested coyly.

Was he asking me out, or simply propositioning me for more sex? You know what, I was up for both, so I replied positively.

We stayed on the red blanket all afternoon. Ben decorated my naked body in wild flowers: daisies, dandelions, buttercups and clover. He made me feel so special; we made love again and I didn't want the day to end. I was surprised no one had passed us, either on foot or on the river, or maybe they had and we simply hadn't noticed. This made me laugh, can you imagine rowing your boat along the river and seeing two naked bodies up on the river bank? Bit of a surprise I would have thought, or maybe not.

It was the end of the afternoon and it was starting to get chilly. We both got dressed, packed away the picnic and folded up the blanket. I hugged the blanket as I climbed back into the boat, the softness of it and the smell of sex on it made me feel warm and cosy; I didn't want to let go, holding on to the moment as long as I could.

Ben rowed the boat back to the boathouse; I did offer, but he pointed out that as we were travelling upstream it would be pretty tough going. I wasn't going to argue so lay back on the seat. As we got closer to town the river was much busier and noisier. Lots of boats were out, bumping into each other going this direction and that. It all seemed pretty chaotic and a big contrast from the serene boat trip we'd just had.

It was nice to see so many couples and families out on a Sunday afternoon on the river. It was at times like that I really appreciated English eccentricities. We arrived at the boathouse and Ben and I climbed out of the boat with our belongings.

"Hi Ben, had a good trip?" a guy working the boats shouted out.

"Awesome!" Ben replied. I smiled smugly to myself, *he's referring to me!* I thought, *he thinks my company is awesome!* I was grinning like a Cheshire cat.

We walked away from the boathouse holding hands. I couldn't quite believe what had happened that afternoon. It had been amazing and wonderful. Amazing, wonderful and Dandelion Jensen were an unusual combination of words to say the least. Dandelion Jensen's life does not usually contain those adjectives. Things were looking up, whatever happened now, we would always have that afternoon.

My phone rang, it was Ash. "Hi," I said.

"Dandie, have you been in touch with Mum?" he asked. *Hi Ash, yes, I'm fine thank you, I've had a simply magical day on the river with the most gorgeous man I've ever met.* As if Ash would ever actually be interested in me or my life.

"No, have you?" I replied.

"No, I'm going over, d'you want to come?" he asked.

The thought of Ash going round to Mum's without me sent a shiver through me. He was sure to burst in there with the subtlety of a sledgehammer. I had to go with him.

"Yes, can you pick me up on the way?" I answered, a little reluctantly.

"Yeah, sure, in five?"

"No, Ash, I'm not at home. Can you give me forty mins?"
Ash let out a big sigh, patience was not one of his virtues.
"OK, see you in forty."

Well my nice cosy bubble just went 'pop'!
"Trouble?" Ben asked.
"Family stuff," I replied. "I've got to go home and meet my brother."
"OK, Dandie, thanks for a great day. Can we do it again sometime?"
"Thank you Ben! Yes, I would love to," I replied excitedly. "I've got to go now."
We stood entwined in a passionate embrace on the pavement. I really didn't want to go.
"See you soon," Ben said. I turned back as I walked away.
"You bet!" I replied, smiling.

I wanted to jump and skip down the road, but fearing that might look strange to onlookers, I sufficed with giggling out loud to myself. I had a date, I think. Dandelion Jensen may have a boyfriend. I felt so happy. Today had been truly remarkable and so special. Ben was such a great guy; we'd had a wonderful time together and I really hoped there would be more to follow.

Then, back down to reality and the decidedly unromantic Ash. I was anxious about what the next few hours would offer. I was concerned about Mum as I hadn't had any contact with her since we left her the day before with Tom Bradley. What had gone on between them I had no idea. I hoped she was ok; I really hoped that her meeting with Tom had provided some happy resolution.

Chapter thirty

As I reached my home, Ash was already standing on the doorstep. This was typical of Ash. If it was in his mind to do something, everyone had to drop everything and act immediately. Somehow though the same rules didn't seem to apply in reverse. If you wanted Ash to be somewhere at a particular time, you could guarantee that he would be late.

"Where have you been?" he asked, impatiently.
"Hot date on the river!" I replied, winking at him.
He looked confused. It either didn't register, or he hadn't even taken in what I had said.
"Come upstairs Ash, I've got a couple of things to do first."
Ash shuffled irritably and reluctantly followed me up the stairs to my flat.
"What's the hurry?" I asked him when we were inside.
"I don't know, I just want to check she's ok. Is that all right by you?" he asked defensively.
"OK, chill!" I replied. "How was your little tête-à-tête with Tom Bradley yesterday?" I asked as I was genuinely interested.

"Yeah, it was cool. He's a pretty cool guy. We could do worse for a long-lost brother." He said, smiling. His thoughtfulness seemed to have distracted him a little and I was relieved by this.
"Tell me more," I replied.
"On the way. Come on Dandie, I've been hanging around for ages."
"Ok, ok. Just give me a sec to get ready!"
"Jeez Louise!" Ash retorted and started drumming on the table top annoyingly.

I made him a cup of tea and had a quick shower. I was still covered in bits of grass and flowers. It seemed a shame to wash it all away as I wanted to savour the memory for a little longer.

I emerged clean and refreshed and put on a change of clothes. Ash by this point was pacing up and down across my living room.

"Ash you're going to wear the carpet out!"

"Jeez Dandie, how long does it take a girl to get ready? We're only going to the 'rents!"

"Ok, almost ready. Chill!" I grabbed my bag and we left the flat, feeling decidedly hassled, *cheers for that Ash!*

As we walked to the parked car, the sky began to cloud over. For the first time in a week the sun was beginning to hide. When we were in the car we drove past my building on the way to Mum and Dad's. We drove over the exact spot of the accident, but there was no sign whatsoever of the crash; it were as if it had never happened. I gave a brief thought to the poor lorry driver. All attention had been focused on Tom Bradley, but I knew nothing of the whereabouts or condition of the lorry driver and I really hoped he was ok. It occurred to me also, that we still didn't really know the cause of the crash. I must get in touch with Charley and see if she could shed any light on it all via Beth, but that would have to wait for now.

I felt a bit nervous about visiting Mum. If it hadn't been for Ash steamrolling the whole situation I'm not sure I would be going to see her yet, as it seemed a bit too soon and too intrusive. However, I didn't feel happy about Ash going on his own as subtlety was not one of his virtues and I didn't want him to say the wrong thing. I knew he wouldn't do anything to purposely upset her, it's just that he could be a

164

bit of a loose cannon. I guess I was tagging along to try and keep him in check. I was also intrigued to find out how the meeting between them had gone.

While we were in the car I asked Ash more about Tom.
"What's he like?" I asked Ash as drove to Mum and Dads.
"Tom? He's pretty cool. Turns out we've got quite a lot in common," Ash replied.
"Oh, like what?" I said, slightly surprised.
"Similar interests; he likes music and it turns out he's not a bad drummer."
"Really?" I said, turning to look at Ash.
"Yeah, and he's quite active, he does a lot of climbing and racing."
"Climbing and racing?"
"Yeah, he climbs up cliffs and rocks. He travels all over searching for ever-more challenging climbs."
"How's that in common with you? You've never climbed anything in your life!"
"Well, I'd like to."
"That's absolute rubbish Ash! If you wanted to you'd have done by now."
"He also likes racing."
"Racing?"
"Yeah, you know, driving fast."

I give up. It seemed like Ash was clinging onto threads, wanting to find something which would bind the two of them together. I looked out of the window wishing in retrospect that I had taken the time to get to know Tom Bradley myself. I felt a bit sad about that, it really did seem like a missed opportunity.

Ash parked the car near our parents' place and we got out and made our way up to their house. As I walked up to the front door, through the garden of wild flowers, I was taken back momentarily to the wonderful afternoon I'd had with Ben. I looked up at the house against the early evening sky; the windows were illuminated with lights and I could hear music playing. We knocked on the door and let ourselves in.

"Hello!" Ash called out. There was no answer. We walked into the front room; the lights were on and the usual chaos greeted us, but no parents. We walked through the back into the kitchen, again no one was around.
"Mum, Dad, anyone home?" I called up the stairs.

I heard loud footsteps coming down the stairs.
"Hello lovely people, what a wonderful surprise!" Dad said loudly as he made his way down to the ground floor. I looked at Ash and said quietly, "You did tell them we were coming didn't you?"
"May have forgotten that bit," he replied, sheepishly.

"Tea, coffee, whiskey?" Dad offered, after giving both Ash and myself a great big bear hug.
We followed him into the kitchen where he prepared the drinks.
"How's Mum?" I asked.
Dad didn't answer immediately and we waited in silence for his reply. After a few seconds he turned around to us both.

"Sylvie's ok, but it's all been a bit much for her, she's resting at the moment," he said in uncharacteristic seriousness. We all sat down together at the long pine kitchen table and he sat down with us and reached out a hand to each of us. "She needs a bit of time, then she'll be

166

back to herself again. It's so great to see you both, how are you?"

"How did it go at the hospital?" I asked Dad, almost wishing I hadn't.
"Well... you know we almost didn't go? Dad began. "I think Sylvie went for the boys' sake, not her own. I think she felt she owed it to him. She was interested to meet him too, obviously. He seems like a nice lad."

"I really like him," Ash said.
"I'm glad Ash. As I said he's a nice lad and your mother should be proud of him. I'm glad he found us actually and I very much hope we will see more of him. I welcome him into our family with open arms and look forward to getting to know him better. I hope you do too," Dad said.
"Yeah, sure," Ash said. "I have to admit, I was a bit apprehensive at first and I wanted to know what he was after, if he was genuine, but he's ok"
I looked at Ash in disbelief, *'what he was after, was he genuine' seriously Ash!* The poor guy was looking for his family, simple as that.
"Dandie?" Dad said.
"What?" I asked, surprised.
"What do you think?"
"I don't know Dad, I didn't really talk to him. Do you know that Charley met him in Venice?" I was confused and didn't know what to say. I mean is this guy suddenly a part of our family? Dad and Ash seemed to be talking about him as if he was their new best friend. For me there were so many unresolved issues, primarily why we hadn't been told of his existence before and what were Mum's thoughts on all this?

There was a loud knock at the front door and a shrill voice called out:

"Hi Dad, Mum, it's Rose and David."

Not now! I thought to myself and looked helplessly at Ash and Dad.

Dad immediately got up and hurried to the front door, composing himself brilliantly and booming out a warm hello and welcome to them both. Ash and I just looked at each other resigned.

"Come in, come in, how fabulous to see you both. Ash and Dandie are here too. Come on through and I'll make some more drinks."

Chapter thirty one

"Well hello dear siblings," Rose said, coldly. "What a gathering, what brings you both here?"

Ash, Dad and I all looked at each other.

"Ok, what's going on?" Rose asked, not one to wait tactfully. David, on the other hand, sensing something delicate was occurring, quietly suggested they sit down with everyone else at the table. Dad made Rose and David drinks and brought them to the table.

"There you go," Dad said. "How lovely to have everyone here together," he continued, attempting small talk. Rose looked sharply and expectantly at everyone. We all avoided eye contact. She looked at David.

"Well?" she said impatiently. "Where's Mum?" she said suddenly, as though she had only just noticed Mum was not there.

"Mum's upstairs, resting," Dad offered.

"Why what's wrong with her, what's going on? I demand to know what is going on around here?" she said, bossily.

"Mum's fine, Rose, please don't worry. She's had a bit of a shock," Dad said and looked at Ash and me for reassurance. I knew better than to get into a conversation with Rose as it inevitably became more of a battlefield. Ash remained uncharacteristically quiet.

"David," Rose said, as if instructing him to interrogate us all.

"Hmm," David began. "Ok, we have obviously walked into a situation here so would it not be prudent to explain what is going on?"

The silence that followed was deafening, I could hardly bear it. Who and how was anyone going to explain to Rose about Mum and Tom Bradley.

"Oh Rose," Dad started.
"Yes, Dad," she replied, impatiently, but nervously.
"It would appear you have another sibling," he began clumsily.
Rose stood bolt upright in shock. "Dad! How could you?" she exclaimed, angrily. "When, how? Oh poor Mum!"
"No, no, Rose hold your horses. Sit back down and listen for once," he said firmly. I just looked at her in disgust; typical Rose to get the wrong end of the stick as usual, jumping to conclusions without ever finding out the facts.
"Shut up, you idiot!" Ash said coldly to Rose. Even David remained silent, obviously feeling out of his depth.

Dad took a deep breath and had a drink of his whiskey. "Rose, please, sit down and listen," he said more calmly.

"A long time ago, before Sylvie and I met, something happened to your mother." Dad paused, Ash and I simply sat quietly. I was more than happy to watch Dad try to explain everything to Rose. Rose was quiet, but her facial expressions were full of angst. She waited in silence for Dad to continue.
After a deep breath he resumed, "When Sylvie was fifteen she had a 'brief encounter' which produced a baby boy... of whom she knew very little, until the other day when he unexpectedly entered our lives."

Rose let out a small scream, and immediately gasped. She looked at me and then Ash accusingly.
"You knew?" she demanded. I nodded.
"Only a few days ago," was all I could muster to say.

"What the hell!" she replied angrily.

"Rose calm down," David said, firmly.

I wasn't sure if Rose was cross because of what had happened to Mum, or that fact that Ash and I knew about it before she did. I sincerely hoped it was the former, but sadly suspected the latter to be the case.

I heard light footsteps coming down the stairs and Mum entered into the kitchen.

"Hello everyone," she said, surprised. "I thought I heard voices, what is all the shouting about?" she said quietly and calmly. She looked pretty rough and her face was drawn. She was dressed in a kimono gown and her hair was unbrushed.

"We thought you were sleeping," Dad said going up to her and giving her a cuddle.

"I was, but then there was all this noise. My children are here, I'm not going to miss out on a visit," she said smiling.

Rose simply looked at her speechless, almost as if she were a stranger.

"Rose, are you ok?" Mum asked.

Rose didn't reply, she simply sat down.

For once could Rose just think of someone other than herself? I thought frustratingly.

"How are you Mum?" I asked, reaching out my hand.

"Tired Dandie, very, very tired. How are you lovely? What's been going on in Dandie's life?"

I told her about Ben and how we'd had a nice row down the river in a boat. She smiled and seemed genuinely interested and pleased for me. Her attention span was short though, and after a little while she excused herself and went to her room. Dad accompanied her back upstairs.

"What the hell Dandie, why didn't you tell me?" Rose said, angrily.
"Really can't imagine!" Ash interjected, sarcastically.
"Rose, this is not about you," I replied.
She took in a deep breath,
"Ok, what do you know?"
"That's pretty much it," I replied.
"Who's the boy, who's the perpetrator?" Rose demanded.
"You know the accident, outside my flat last week?"
"Yes."
"Well, the guy in the car, Tom Bradley, is the boy mum gave up for adoption."
Rose looked stunned.
"You have got to be kidding, no way. How do you know?"

I filled Rose in with all the details and extraordinary coincidences that Ash and I had encountered over the previous few days. She listened in stunned silence. I concluded with,
"Mum and Dad went to visit Tom Bradley yesterday, so Ash and I came over today to see how it went."
Rose looked perplexed and turned to David for reassurance, not seeming to know quite how to react.
"He's a really nice guy, Rose, you should meet him… on second thoughts, maybe not," Ash added.
"What are you implying Ash?" Rose said, defensively.
"I couldn't possibly comment," he replied.

Chapter thirty two

We sat around the table in silence, Rose, David, Ash and me. Rose's face looked pained as she tried to make sense of all the information she had just received. David looked awkward and uncomfortable, as if he'd much rather not be there. Ash was smouldering. I simply felt worried for Mum. After what seemed like an eternity, Dad reappeared. We all looked at him expectantly.

"Mum's resting, she's very touched you're all here," Dad said, soundly reassuringly upbeat, in stark contrast to the gloomy atmosphere that seemed to hover over the kitchen table.

"Why the grim faces?" Dad asked.
"What the hell!" screeched Rose, explosively. "I've just found out that I have a 'brother', which, it seems, everyone knew about except me!"
"Rose, my dear, please calm down," Dad said calmly. "Nothing was hidden from you alone. Mum chose not to tell anyone, and I mean anyone! None of her friends or family knew of Tom's existence."
"No one?" Rose replied in disbelief.
"No one," Dad firmly replied.
"Not even Granny, Gramp or Aunt Lizzie?"
"Aunt Lizzie, no. Granny and Gramp did find out and took control," Dad replied thoughtfully.
"What your mother went through was extremely difficult for her; it also happened a long time ago. It's very important we all take that into account. We decided, rightly or wrongly, not to tell you all about what had happened, or about Tom Bradley. It was the way your mother chose to deal with the situation and I respected that."

He paused and we sat in silence waiting for him to continue.

"Sylvie felt she didn't have any control over the situation she found herself in. This is not as uncommon as you may like to think. Teenage pregnancies were often hidden from public view with the expectant mother losing control over her baby's future. It's a sad state of affairs and thankfully these days there is more help and support on offer. Anyhow, I digress, the point here is that Sylvie chose to deal with the situation by blocking it out; she was effectively in denial about the whole pregnancy. She was just a child, scared and alone. She didn't know there was help or where to find it. Sylvie has lived with that guilt and it's been very difficult."

Dad got up and paced around the room as we all sat obediently in silence.
"She never held the baby, or even saw him. He was taken away from her immediately and we believe he may have been slightly premature and spent time in an incubator. Sylvie didn't know if Tom Bradley would ever reappear in her life, but we always knew it was a possibility. He had a right to seek her out, after all."

Dad paused again before continuing. "Tom Bradley seems a nice lad. He's been brought up in a loving and close family. He doesn't mean any harm to us, and doesn't want to intrude into our lives. In short he doesn't 'want' anything from us. He needed to know where he came from and I know that it's difficult for you to understand because you know nothing different, but just imagine if you knew that your birth parents were not the people who'd brought you up, wouldn't you be curious? It's like investigating a family tree. You may be fascinated that a distant relative of two hundred years ago was called Doris and if you could, you'd probably like to meet her. It doesn't mean that you want to be part of her life, just that you're interested in her because she's connected to you."

I wasn't quite sure what point Dad was trying to make, but we all listened on as he continued. "As I already said, Mum never saw the baby... she didn't want to. He was taken from her immediately. There was no chance to bond. When we talked about starting our own family, she took a lot of persuading; don't get me wrong, she desperately wanted children, but she was terrified that she would reject them and have no feelings for them. When she gave birth to you, Ash, and first held you in her arms, she was so happy and elated. Not just because you were a beautiful baby, but because she loved you, she bonded with you and she wasn't sure that she would. It was a massive relief and she stopped being scared then."

Dad sat down, he seemed tired and retrospective. For a while no one said a word. "Now that this is all out in the open, I hope we can move on. Nothing has changed and we're all the same people we were. In respect for your mother I would request that we keep our knowledge within the family for now. I'd like for us all to continue our lives as they were."

"You may have known about this for years, but it's all new for us, of course it changes things," Rose said.
"Then may it change things in a positive way dear Rose. We should welcome Tom Bradley into our family with open arms. It's the least we can do," Dad replied.
"Who was it that got Mum pregnant?" Rose said.
"I don't know," Dad replied.
"What? I don't believe you!" Rose retorted.

175

Dad looked at Rose very sternly and Rose sat back realising she'd gone too far.

I felt for Dad, really I did, but for once I found myself agreeing with Rose, though probably for different reasons. Mum and Dad had known about this for thirty years. We needed time to adjust too. Finding out you have another sibling, however exciting that is, is still a bit of a shock. Personally I was coming around to the idea, but then I'd had a day or two head start on Rose.

"I'd just like to add one more very important thing," Dad said, "and that is your mother's feeling very vulnerable right now. This whole episode's brought up so many supressed feelings and emotions. She's exhausted and needs some rest, but she also needs to know that we love her, support her and most importantly – we don't judge her. Meeting Tom yesterday was very overwhelming for her. Just imagine what it must have been like – she'd convinced herself that she felt nothing for him, then she came face to face with him, and all those supressed emotions were released. Thirty odd years of denial, wow!"

I can't imagine what Mum must have been going through these past few days, really I can't. It's difficult because I don't think I'd have done what she did in her situation, why didn't she fight for him?

I'd had enough so I made my excuses and left the house. As I began the long walk home, I felt sad and confused. I tried to see where Dad was coming from. They had built a loving, warm family and home life, and protected us from what had happened in the past, but I couldn't agree with that; I think they made a mistake.

Chapter thirty three

It was good to get out into the open and take in some fresh air. It was getting dark. As I walked along the pavement I tried to put all the angst out of my head. I thought back to the afternoon I'd had with Ben; I smiled to myself and felt warm inside. It had been a beautiful afternoon, and Ben was such a nice guy. I felt very fortunate indeed to have met him.

I had decided that my afternoon with Ben would be the focus of the day and not all the craziness that was going down with my family. I thought I'd give Charley a ring and talk to her while making my way home.

"Charley, hello, how do?" I asked when she picked up my call.

"Dandie, I'm good. Beth's gone, so I'm getting the place back together. What's been happening?"

"Tom's really gone then?" I asked.

"Seems so," Charley replied.

I felt a little saddened by that. I wish I'd made more of an effort to get to know him. I wondered if we'd meet again and guessed it would be pretty likely now he'd made the connection.

I told Charley all about my night out with Jacinta and the girls, and also about the wonderful day I'd had with Ben.

"No way!" Charley exclaimed. "Who's this Ben? I have to meet him!" she said excitedly.

"Haha, I'm sure you will, sometime. You'll like him, he's really cool," I said happily. "Also, I've booked a holiday to Venice!"

"No way!" Charley replied. "Dandie, you've been very busy this weekend!"

Charley was right, it had been an extraordinary weekend, well week really.

"Dandie, you are going to have an amazing time in Venice! I can give you loads of tips on where to go, I'm so excited for you," Charley said.

For the second time today, I felt very happy indeed. It had been an emotional day, there was no doubt about it. I didn't feel like going home as I had too much going on in my head so I suggested popping in on Charley, and as she was up for it, I made a detour to her place.

Charley's was a fun place to be. She made some tea, served in fine bone china tea cups and saucers. I asked her how it had been having Beth around. Charley said that she hadn't seen much of her as she'd spent most of the time at the hospital with Tom Bradley.

"She's pleasant enough," Charley said, "but it was difficult circumstances, and very awkward."

"What did she say about you and Tom Bradley being in Venice?" Charley looked a little embarrassed.

"We didn't really talk about it. She did ask, but I just kind of shrugged it off as a very bizarre coincidence. I told her that we'd spent time together with him showing me around. I also added that he spoke very highly of his girlfriend!"

"But you told me he hardly mentioned her!"

"A white lie to get her off the scent. Really Dandie, nothing untoward happened. I think I probably read more into the situation than I should have. Thinking back he was only being nice and was probably pleased to show someone around from England."

Charley was probably right, after all Tom Bradley did seem a decent sort of guy. I paused thoughtfully.

"Charley, did Beth mention my mum at all?" I guess I was fishing on Beth's angle.

"Hmm, yes she did, a bit," Charley replied, hesitantly.

She got up and selected some records on the jukebox. I laughed at her diligence to fight against the banality of modern technology. She truly was the only person I knew who listened to music that way, and I loved her for it.

"Don't you get bored of the same of tunes?" I asked.

Charley laughed in a care-free way.

"No, you do know I can change them whenever I want to, don't you Dandie?"

"Oh, I suppose so, never thought about really."

"So, you were out last night with Josh Kane, you lucky thing you!" Charley said, star struck.

"You know, he was just a regular guy and after the initial 'wow' factor, he seemed very down to earth and, well, ordinary. You'd have liked him, it's a shame you weren't there," I said, thoughtfully.

"Too right it's a shame I wasn't there!"

"Charley, what did Beth say about Mum... and Tom Bradley?" I asked, cautiously, almost not wanting to hear her answer.

"Beth told me that her boyfriend, 'Venice' Tom (seriously, how bizarre is that!) was searching for his birth mother. Apparently he'd been thinking about it for a while. It wasn't a really big deal, just something he wanted to do. I think his sister had found her birth mother and that sort of spurred him on. Anyhow, he didn't have much luck at all as I don't think he had much to go on. To cut to the chase, somehow he connected with Sylvie. I still can't believe it, Dandie."

"Me neither." I replied.

"Wow, did no one know?" she asked.

"Nope, none of us knew until a few days ago. Dad knew obviously, but they hadn't told us."

"It's a pretty huge skeleton to keep in the closet."

"You're telling me!" I replied.

"I got the impression that Tom wanted to contact Ash."

"Yep, he'd got in touch with him, but Ash had thought it was a wind up and hadn't given it much credence."

"So, how did it all go?" Charley asked.

"Hmm, I don't know Charley. I want my old life back, the one I had before last week, the uncomplicated one. You know the weirdest thing of all for me is that I just didn't think of my mum as having a 'past', it's all a bit hard to get my head around."

I wondered then about how cool it would be to have a time machine and travel back in time to the beginning of last week, to start all over again.

I hung out at Charley's for a couple of hours and it was good to have a chance to catch up. She confided in me that after the initial excitement of seeing Tom and realising he was in fact the guy she had spent such a nice time in Venice with, she had quickly come around to the fact that he was her cousin's boyfriend, and they were very close. She was sad about that definitely; I think she had hoped that Tom and her relationship would develop into something deeper, had circumstances been different.

Apart from that we didn't really talk much more about anything related to Tom Bradley. I got the feeling that Charley was pleased he and Beth had left and she had her flat to herself again.

Charley knocked some food together and we sat and ate, and giggled about my night out and the fab time I'd had on the river with the gorgeous Ben. It was girly chat time, good times and the best therapy ever! My advice to anyone, if you feel like life is pulling you along this way and that, have a get together with a good friend. Everything will be clear again.

Chapter thirty four

I left Charley's feeling refreshed, relaxed and relieved. You can't put a price on quality time with good friends. It was Sunday night and a good sleep was in order, before the rush of Monday morning and the daily routine of work and all. Sometimes I think there's a lot to be said for routine and the normality of it as I'd seriously had enough of surprises lately. I'd settle for routine very happily. Yep, I was going to focus on the positive events of the weekend, of which there were many, and not focus on the negative, of which there were also many! Jeez, how I longed for the mundane to return to my life.

Monday morning arrived, I sat on my sofa, coffee in hand, clothed in my dressing gown and stared blankly at the news. What the weather was going to do was really all I was interested in. I ordered blue skies and sunshine and the forecast did not disappoint. Equilibrium restored I continued to get up and embrace the day. Embrace sounds a little tactile, don't you think? (Maybe embattle was more appropriate). Whichever verb was best suited, I was prepared.

As I sat on the bus to work Ben texted me. Oh joy of joys, what a fab start to the day, I was really liking this guy and the way he operated. It was a simple, "Good morning gorgeous" text, but it made me beam from ear to ear. I felt self-conscious of my 'Cheshire cat' expression and had to turn my head towards the window, so I could wallow in the cosy self-satisfied happiness I felt, without people staring at me.

I got to my desk and was greeted by a typically enthused Jade. She had tales of wedding dress shopping, and a huge amount of photographic evidence for me to endure. I was happy for her, really I was, and her excitement was truly infectious. I couldn't help wondering what part, if any, Mike had in all this preparation. I got the feeling that Mike was simply and 'extra' in Jade's great play of life. He was either incredibly devoted to Jade, or lazy, I couldn't make out which. Obviously, for her sake, I hoped the former and to be fair I didn't think there was much doubt.

"Dandelion, just look at all those frills! Oh I nearly wet myself when I saw that one, and look at this beauty, have you ever seen such a poufy skirt? I felt like a princess wearing that one. Look at the size of these puffed sleeves, I thought I'd float away in that. Oh Dandelion, it was the best day of my life, it I felt like I was in a real-life Disney film, really I did. This one here, you'd never guess the petticoats underneath." And so she went on as I had a detailed running commentary on each dress in each photo. I thought her dress had already been chosen and that this visit was just a fitting, but silly me. I was more horrified with each description, and completely overcome with visions of over-the-top meringues and synthetic satin. My idea of a wedding dress couldn't be more opposite. If I were to ever get married, I pictured myself in an elegant simple, silk 'thirties-style number with a small understated train.

However, I was not about to get married any time soon, and Jade most definitely was. So I went along with her euphoria, and you know what, I was genuinely happy for her. It meant so much to her, it was her big day, and she was loud and proud about it. I admired her for that, and flattered that she shared it with me.

The day passed uneventfully, much to my relief. Normality reigned good and strong on this Monday. On the bus home my thoughts drifted back to Ben and our wonderful day together. I wanted to see him again, I really liked him. We hadn't made any definite plans about meeting up. I wanted to call him, but felt oddly shy. I could text him, a little safer? He texted me this morning after all, so I would simply be replying. Sorted, I texted him a simple reply, 'Good evening gorgeous' and left it at that to see what would happen next.

Sure enough, he texted right back which made me giggle. I swear that any people travelling on my bus regularly must think me a giggling goon, but that's ok. Ben asked me when we could meet up again. I wanted to say 'now', but thought I should play it a bit cool. We agreed to meet midweek. I was happy.

When I got home there was an envelope waiting for me. I opened it up, it contained a card, one of Dad's artwork. He'd written inside that he and Mum had decided to go away for a few days. They'd booked a last minute B&B on the coast. It was a brief message, but basically mum was upset and needed a major change of scene. I was relieved and it sounded like a great idea to me. Dad always knew the best way to cheer people up.

My thoughts drifted back to Tom Bradley. I decided that I had acted badly. I decided that I was going to make up for my behaviour and make amends. If I was to reassure Mum that there was no judgement made against her, then surely the way forward was to welcome Tom into our family.

Then I thought, maybe he didn't want to be part of our family. Maybe he was satisfied with just meeting us, and that was all he needed. I was so confused as to what the right thing was to do.

I decided that I would write him a letter, apologising for my rude behaviour, and letting him know that I would be happy to meet him again, if he wanted to. I hoped Mum wouldn't mind. Then again, as it was all out in the open, at least within the immediate family, surely we were at liberty to now form our own relationships with our new found brother? You know, after the initial shock, I was seriously coming around to the idea of having another family member. I was keen to find out more about him and about his family and his sister. The situation was taking on an altogether exciting new direction.

Chapter thirty five

It was Tuesday, again. This day, one week ago, my life changed unexpectedly. What a difference a day makes, a bit corny I know, but it's true. This Tuesday was passing quietly and uneventfully, much to my relief.
As I was ambling along on my way home, thinking of nothing in particular, my phone rang. It was Sol and that made me smile.

"Hi Dandie, how are you?" he asked.
"I'm cool and you?" I replied.
"Yeah, I'm cool. Listen up Dandie, remember that gig I mentioned to you? You never said if you wanted to go or not. It's tomorrow night, what do you reckon?"
"Oh Sol, I completely forgot to get back to you. I have plans tomorrow night, sorry."
Sol laughed. "No worries," he said, I guess he'd already realised it wasn't going to happen. I like Sol, really I do. I like spending time with him and he's a good friend. It took a while for us to become friends after we'd split up, but we got there in the end. We don't meet up often, but when we do, it's nice as it feels comfortable and familiar. He's become like another brother to me. We have a bond and a lot of shared memories and experiences which can never be taken away and will always tie us together.

He was doing really well professionally, like I always knew he would as he's very driven. Funnily enough, like me, he hadn't really had a long-term relationship since we broke up all those years ago. I was surprised about that as he was a great catch for the right woman. He had everything going for him; lovely personality, good looking, comfortably off. Maybe he just didn't want a serious relationship again.

Maybe I'd scarred him for life. Or maybe, as some people have suggested, he still held a torch for me. I couldn't give that idea much credence, I mean, seriously, why me? Dandelion Jensen, the girl no one notices.

Anyhow, I had a date with boatman Ben on Wednesday and there was nothing that could compete with that.

"Did you ever find out any more about that Tom Bradley guy?" Sol asked, genuinely interested.

"Haha, yes Sol, quite a lot, but you probably wouldn't believe any of it," I replied.

"Try me, I'm intrigued."

"Let's just say he has a lot of connections with a lot of people around here, who'd have known, eh?"

"Sounds interesting, spill."

"One day I will Sol, right now it's a bit complicated to talk about over the phone."

"Funny old world isn't it?" Sol replied.

"Sure is. Sol, I would like to meet up with you soon, it's been a long time. Maybe coffee one day?" I offered, feeling a bit bad letting him down on the whole gig thing.

"Sounds good to me. Give me a shout when you're free ok."

"Will do, enjoy the gig," I said.

"Enjoy the date," he replied.

"How did you know I had a date?" I replied, surprised.

"Dandie, you're as transparent as a pane of glass?" Sol laughed and signed off.

I smiled thinking of my impending date with Ben and wondered what he had in mind for the evening. I was also pleased that Sol had got in touch; he meant a lot to me and it had taken quite a while for our friendship to reach this level. I had a lot of respect and time for Sol.

Wednesday came around in a flash. I was meeting Ben and I was excited about that. Ben had asked me round to his place and he was going to cook me dinner. A man that can cook, had this man no faults? It turned out that Ben's place was not far from the boathouse on the river side, but you can only get that way by boat. On foot, it is a longer way around by road, which kind of loops around and back on itself before you get to the entrance. It was a funny building, a bit like a loft and very old, Tudor possibly. It stood on big old wooden stilts with a rickety staircase going up around the side of the building. It was all on one level and consisted of one medium-sized room with vaulted ceiling, with a small bedroom and bathroom leading off to one side. The main room was living, kitchen and dining room all in one. Windows looked out over the river. It was quirky and interesting, though not the cleanest place I've visited. The windows were made up of twelve small panes each which were so grubby you could hardly see out of them. Up in the rafters were large well-established cobwebs. However the table, chairs and floor were spotless so I think he'd had a tidy up before I arrived.

The food smelled delicious. He had prepared a wonderful meal of a Provençal pie with a Mediterranean salad. The table was candle lit and we opened the bottle of white wine I'd brought along. We both sat down to eat. It sounds so cheesy, but it really was incredibly romantic. The window was slightly open and I could hear the gentle flow of the river below. The food tasted incredible.

"Wow, Ben you can cook!"
"Thank you Dandie, glad you like it. I enjoy cooking and experimenting with food and recipes."
"Do you have any faults?" I asked, teasingly.

"Haha, you'll have to make up your own mind about that," was his evasive response.

"This place is amazing Ben, how did you get to live here?" I asked, looking around the room.

"Comes with the job, I'm very lucky," he replied.

I looked at him, his life, his home and said thoughtfully, "Yeah you really are."

"Haha, to have you?" he asked.

"No, no I didn't mean it like that!" I replied, embarrassed, realising how that may have been misinterpreted.

"Well, actually I think I am very lucky to have you?" he said, leaning over the table and holding my hand.

"Oh, so you 'have' me do you?" I replied, teasing.

"I hope so," he said. "Hopefully long term rather than on temporary loan."

"You make me sound like a possession!" I protested.

"Possession? No. Friend, lover, soul-mate, yes, I hope so. I meant for keeps, rather than just a passing fling. What do you think?"

I was a little overcome with flattery and didn't know quite how to respond. Ben certainly knew how to make a girl feel special. I was completely swept away by him.

"Sounds like an acceptable proposal to me," was the best response I could come up with. I thought it a bit lame, but hey.

We had a lovely evening in his romantic loft, with candle light, wine and the sounds of the river. I was in a very happy place indeed. So much so that I couldn't quite believe it was happening to me.

Chapter thirty six

I woke up to the sound of the birds singing outside on the river bank. Rays of sunlight shone diagonally across the bedroom, catching the iron rods of Ben's bedstead. I looked at him as he slept. He looked so peaceful and calm. His dark curls surrounding his head like a halo. I got up to make some coffee. It was quite cold and draughty, so I quickly put on some clothes to keep warm. As I lifted the latch on the bedroom door and pulled it open, it creaked loudly. I looked at Ben who stirred slightly, but didn't wake.

I opened the window wide and leaned out, clasping a hot cup of coffee in my hands. I looked out over the river below. There were no buildings to be seen, just the flowing water and grass bank with weeping willows hanging and trailing gracefully into the water. There were a clump of water lilies in flower just opposite. The water was a green-brown colour, but still fairly clear. It seemed quite deep as I couldn't make out the river bed, but could see fish swimming around just below the surface. Where the sunlight caught and reflected off the ripples of water it was so bright that it was almost blinding.

I felt a little envious of Ben's life; it seemed so peaceful.
"Well there's a vision you can't beat in the morning," Ben said.
"Oh, you made me jump!" I exclaimed. He came over and joined me looking out of the window.
"Not a bad view eh?" he said.
"You're a very lucky man," I said again. He grabbed hold of me and pulled me towards him in a gentle embrace.

"I know I am, look what I've got in my arms," he said and kissed me passionately on the lips.

He lured me back to bed and the morning was made even more perfect, as we gently caressed and had fabulous sex.

Yay, I was well set up for the day and really didn't want to spoil it all by going to work. Just think, if I hadn't taken last Tuesday off but taken today off instead, how much happier my life would be. Hindsight is indeed a wonderful thing and if I were equipped with the ability to time travel, the two would make an awesome combination. Unfortunately, back in reality, without time travel I had to get to work before I was late. Ben too, had to get ready for work, so together we breakfasted and said our goodbyes.

As I walked down the rickety wooden stairs to ground level and the noise of the traffic outside, it felt as though I were entering a parallel universe. Being at Ben's place really did seem dreamlike, a world away and yet so close. Could I really be lucky enough to be welcomed into his world, on a permanent arrangement? I felt like pinching myself to make sure this was all really happening and not just a fantastic dream. Strange times indeed. I really didn't want to leave and hoped I would be invited back very soon. I kind of thought I might be.

I got to work, but with all the will in the world found it impossible to focus. I kept thinking about what an amazing evening I'd had with Ben. I found myself being jealous of me! How bizarre is that? Even Jade's full on gossiping couldn't distract me.

I was happy in my bubble of contentedness. I almost felt immune to hassle and strife. Ben made me feel so special.

My phone rang. It was Rose, I could handle her, I was invincible I told myself as I answered her call.

"Dandelion!" she said in her typical unfriendly manner.
"Rose." I replied calmly.
"We need to meet," she continued.
"We do?" I replied, uninterested. Seriously I couldn't be bothered with whatever drama she was about to create.
"Yes we do, we have things to discuss, family things. I won't repeat them on the phone, but you know exactly what I'm talking about. I'm calling a meeting with you, Ash and myself. I have a twenty-minute window this lunchtime. I expect to see you both at 1pm sharp at the Chocolate Café." With that she hung up, without as much as a courteous goodbye.

My bubble remained intact, not even Rose could burst it. I obviously had no intention of meeting up with Rose, I had far better things to do with my time than spend it with someone so rude, self-obsessed and demanding. Besides the Chocolate Café was such a lovely place I didn't want to share any time there with someone as toxic as Rose, she would ruin its magic.
Soon after Rose's call I got a call from Ash.

"Ahhhh!" he said down the phone, I laughed.
"Haha, she phoned you too," I said.
"Seriously who is she, where does she get off bossing everyone around? Jeez she's an expert at winding people up and pissing them off!"
"I guess you're not meeting up with her then?" I replied.
"Too right I'm not. She has no idea how to interact with people. You know if she had said something along the lines of 'it would be lovely to all meet up, when are you

both free?' it would have at least been a start. Seriously who does she think she is?"

"Don't let her get to you Ash, we can't let her bully us into things."

"I know Dandie, but she makes me mad, really she does. I don't know how David puts up with her."

"Ash, I had the most wonderful night last night, I stayed at Ben's place, it's amazing. You'd love it. I had the best time, and you know what, it really made me realise how being around some people can have such a positive effect on you. Don't waste any energy on negative people like Rose, it's simply not healthy. Anyhow, are you free this lunch time, I'd like to know more about Tom Bradley?"

"Sure. Always have time for my little sis'."

We arranged to meet.

Chapter thirty seven

Lunch time came and I managed to get an hours' break. I made my way to the pub to find Ash already there.

"Wow, you're on time," I said.

"Yes," Ash replied, confused by my statement. "You still smiling?" he continued.

"Oh yes, I'm holding on to this happy feeling for as long as I can!" I replied. We ordered some ploughman's and sat down at a table in a window alcove.

As I started tucking into my food Ash began talking about the recent events.

"You know Dandie, I was seriously apprehensive about Tom at first."

"No kidding," I replied, thinking *understatement of the year*. "You were so aggressive, Ash."

"I know, ok kid, I'm not proud of it. It was just all a bit of a shock. I guess I was feeling protective of Mum. You know, I didn't know the facts, I didn't know if he was for real."

"What do you mean 'for real'? He wasn't a robot!" I laughed.

"You know what I'm getting at Dandie, he could have been a fraud. I was suspicious about his motives."

I shamefully had to admit to sharing some of Ash's concerns. In hindsight Ash had behaved better than I. At least he made an effort to get to know Tom Bradley. I was disappointed that I hadn't.

"What's he like?" I asked, genuinely interested.

"He's cool, really he is. He had a definite advantage in that he knew a lot about us already, and we didn't even know he existed. I got the impression that he just wanted to satisfy his curiosity. From what he said, he had a great family life and is close to his dad and sister. He's interesting too. His conservation work sounded cool, seems he's spent a lot of time in Italy and can even speak fluent Italian. Puts me to shame really." Ash paused thoughtfully. "You know I'd like to meet him again. We should invite him down to stay once he's fully recovered, that'd be a cool thing to do."

"Hold up Ash, what about Mum?"

"Hmm, hadn't thought of that." We sat quietly thinking and eating for a few minutes.

"Couldn't we build our own relationship with him, he is after all, our half-brother?" Ash said.

Half-brother, jeez that sounded so weird and was going to take some getting used to. I wasn't entirely convinced that Ash's enthusiasm wasn't a little premature. I needed to know how Mum was and what her thoughts were.

"What about Tom's biological father?" I asked.

"What about him?" Ash replied.

"Haven't you thought about him?"

"No? Why should I?"

"I don't know. It's just hard to get my head around the fact that out there somewhere is a middle-aged man who has an, albeit very nice, son whom he doesn't even know exists."

"Dandie, if you think about it, there are probably loads of guys who've unknowingly fathered offspring; I may have even."

I looked at Ash in shock.

"Ash, are you trying to tell me something?"

"Of course not little sis, but you know, it's possible."

I sat back in my chair and looked around at all the men in the pub. *Have any of them unknowingly fathered a child?* What a ridiculous thing to think, I told myself.

"Tom must have thought about it," I said.

"I guess," Ash replied, showing more interest in the remains of his ploughman's than my conversation.

I found it really hard to believe that Mum had no idea at all. Was she still hiding information from us all?

Chapter thirty eight

Mine and Ash's phones rang simultaneously; it was Rose, we both hit the reject button.

"Dandie, all this talk about Tom has been a bit of a distraction. Seems some guy's been paying you attention. Tell me more about 'Ben'." Ash said changing the subject.

Wow, Ash was actually interested in my life, this was new. I felt overcome with embarrassment and could feel myself blushing self-consciously. I let out an impulsive school girl giggle.

"I don't know what to tell. He's called Ben, he works on the boats, he lives in a wonderful loft house, and I think he's my boyfriend!" I replied.

"Cool, maybe we could all meet up?"

"Yes, that would be good."

With that we said our goodbyes and I ran back to work, just making it in time.

I felt invincible with my happy bubble still intact, despite Rose's efforts to burst it. Finding myself in a surprisingly positive state of mind somehow gave an incredible clarity to my thoughts. Instead of feeling intimidated by the whole Tom Bradley situation, I found myself wanting to know more about him, and reflecting on how incredibly brave he was to have sought us out. I was not proud of my behaviour towards him and I could have made much more of an effort to be welcoming instead of being so hostile. Ultimately though, my thoughts kept drifting back to the wonderful Ben. I was blown away by how good he made me feel. I hadn't felt this way for such a long time, and it felt good, really good. I thought about my trip to Venice.

How cool would it be if Ben came too? Was it too soon though, we'd only known each other a week after all?

Finally the work day was over and I had completely glazed over Jade's elaborate musings. For once my life was more interesting than hers. I was looking forward to being at home. I felt as though I hadn't spent much time there and needed some 'me chill out time'. As soon as I arrived back at my flat I changed out of my work clothes into some lounge wear, made a cup of tea and sat down at the table to look over all my Venice plans. I counted the money again, just to reassure myself I hadn't imagined it. I had dreamed about visiting Venice for as long as I could remember and I've read so many books and seen countless programs about it. I couldn't quite believe that I was actually going to go there. How exciting was that!

The evening passed uneventfully, relaxed and cosy.

I woke up a little confused as to where I was. I think I had hoped, or dreamed, that I was at Ben's place again. It was a little disappointing to realise that I was, in fact, in my own bed. I got up, mentally readjusted to my surroundings and the comforting morning routine played out as usual.

As I sat on the sofa, in my dressing gown, cradling my cup of coffee I thought of Mum. I wondered how she was feeling right now. I cared about her deeply; she was just the most kind and thoughtful person I have ever come across. She always put other people's happiness first, no matter what. Even if she was having a really bad day, she would never utter a word about it, she was only ever concerned about making sure everyone else was having a good time. She was completely non-judgemental and one hundred per cent dependable. This was the first time that I could ever remember knowing that she was the one suffering. Her way of dealing with it was typical of her nature, not to bother anyone with her issues, but to go away quietly for a few days. Admittedly it was Dad who'd taken her away, but he'd have done it because he'd have known that was what she would have liked.

I don't think it was to protect us, I really believe it was so as not to bother us. Whatever, I was worried about her. I wanted to see her, just to check on her. It was Friday today, they would surely be home by now. I decided to text Dad first. Unusually he didn't text right back.

I arrived at work to pandemonium. Major wedding plan dramas were going down in the Jade camp.
"Dandelion, you'll never guess what's happened!" she blurted out as soon as I arrived at my desk.

I paused for thought for a second: *Mike's changed his mind about marrying her, the church has burned down, one of the bridesmaids has broken her leg.* "What's happened Jade?" preparing myself for the worst.

"The florists can only provide yellow flowers. Yellow! They were supposed to be purple, the bridesmaids' dresses are all purple! It's always been purple. I said to Mike, they were always purple. Right from the start I told him, purple!" she said, helplessly.
I was trying really hard to be sympathetic and try to understand how this could possibly by Mike's fault.

"Did Mike order the flowers?" I asked.
Jade looked at as if I had just asked a really stupid question. "Dandelion, really dear Dandelion. Of course Mike didn't order the flowers," Jade said this in such a manner as to

imply that the suggestion that Mike would have anything to do with ordering the flowers would have been preposterous, which, knowing Jade I should have guessed really.

Which just left me confused as to how the blame seemed to have been placed on poor old Mike. She continued, there was no stopping Jade once she got going.

"I don't know what to do, I said to Mike 'what am I to do?'" she said. I really can't help feeling for Mike. I wanted to go and rescue him and take him to the pub for a much needed, and earned pint.

"I can't change the dresses now can I? Mum, Aunt Jane and Aunt Julie are ringing around all the other florists looking for purple flowers. Why did they say they could do purple when they couldn't do purple?" Jade continued. Poor Jade, she was very upset.

"Yellow goes quite well with purple," I helpfully suggested.

Jade just gave me another one of her looks.

"Dandelion, I know you mean well, but yellow isn't purple."

I had to agree with Jade, there was no denying it, yellow wasn't purple. I quietly thought to myself that if it were my wedding I would much prefer yellow flowers than purple, but as I knew only too well, this was Jade's wedding; I don't even think of it as Mike and Jade's.

I sat at my desk and tried to concentrate on my work. This wasn't easy with Jade's hysteria going on beside me and the constant phone calls from her matriarchal family about the flower crisis.

I turned to dreaming about my wedding, if I ever had one. What flowers would I have? I think I would like wild flowers. So many flowers these days seemed to have been almost manufactured to perfection, and have lost their natural quality. I have noticed that various types of flowers have lost their scent. Personally I think this is a great shame as flowers are as much about their scent as they are their bloom. I would have a simple posy of wild flowers picked from my parents' garden. Better still, my fiancé would chose and pick the flowers. Oh, how very different my wedding would be to Jade's.

"We could have plastic flowers," I heard Jade suggest over the phone. I nearly fell off my chair, she couldn't possibly be serious, could she?

After several hours and no office work being done that I could see, Jade had finally resolved the flower situation. "Aunt Julie has found a florist that can do purple!" Jade announced triumphantly. Thank goodness for that, drama over.

"When you get married Dandelion I'll help you with all the organising. I think you'll need help Dandelion. It'll be fun," Jade stated, in a matter of fact way. She smiled, clearly pleased with herself that her little crisis had been resolved to her satisfaction.
"Thank you," was the most polite response I could give.
"Have you told Mike about the flowers?" I asked, admittedly, rather provocatively.
Jade gave me another 'look', and smiled. "Mike doesn't need to know," she laughed.
Poor Mike, was all I could think. If I were his friend I think I might advise him to escape while he still had the chance.

Jade got us both some coffee, completely changed the conversation and started talking domestic appliances to me.

I swear she would make an excellent salesperson as she seriously had a knack of making the most boring and trivial item seem the most exciting thing ever, which one couldn't possibly live without. Her talent had no bounds. I looked at her and burst out laughing.

"What?" she asked, surprised by my reaction.
"Nothing Jade, you're just so brilliant. Don't ever change."
She seemed quite flattered and a little flustered by my comment. After a couple of seconds, she coughed politely and continued talking to me about fridges, with unparalleled enthusiasm. She made me smile.

I got a text, it was Dad. He apologised for not replying earlier, but they'd been out of mobile reception, but they were on their way home.

Chapter thirty nine

On my way home from work, my thoughts drifted back to Ben. Would it be cool to ring him? I wanted to see him; it was Friday night and I didn't have work the next day. I loved spending the night in his fab loft house, away from the noise and hecticness of twenty-first century life. I thought about it, I know he'd pretty much made all the moves, so I guess it was my turn.

I went to phone him, when I was suddenly overcome with shyness. *He's probably busy*, I convinced myself and headed home. I wasn't very good at all this dating malarkey and I was so out of practice, I'd forgotten the rules of play, if such a thing even existed. I didn't want to appear too keen, but at the same time I didn't want him to think I wasn't interested. I decided to phone Charley instead.

"Hey Charley, how's your day?" I asked.
"Hello Dandie, things are good, it's Friday after all." Charley replied. Although these words coming from Charley don't necessarily translate the same way as they do for other people, in that being a reporter, there is no such thing as the Monday to Friday nine-to-five routine which we escape from every weekend.

"What are you up to this evening?" she asked.
"Nothing, I'm free," I replied.
"Come over, I'll get some wine in and we can watch a film, how does that sound?" she asked.
"Perfect." I replied. I was looking forward to a girly evening drinking and gossiping with Charley.

Just before I left the flat to head over to Charley's I gave Mum a ring to see how she was.

"Oh Dandie, darling, how lovely to hear from you. How are you?" Mum said.

"I'm good, how are you feeling... after everything?" I asked cautiously. Mum paused before answering.

"I'm fine darling. It's all been a bit of a surprise really. Are you free tomorrow, can I treat you to a drink and cake at the Chocolate Café?" she asked.

"I would love that." I replied and we made arrangements to meet up the following morning.

When I got to Charley's she greeted me with a glass of wine.

"Cheers," she said.

We chatted about this and that and then I thought about Charley spending the week with Tom Bradley in Venice.

"Charley, finding out the Venice Tom was your cousin's boyfriend must have blown your mind?" I asked.

"Pretty much," Charley replied. "Just goes to show doesn't it, how you can misinterpret things. I really liked him you know," she said thoughtfully, looking a little sad.

"I'm sorry," I said.

"Ha it's not your fault Dandie," she replied, "It's just a shame. He's a really great guy, you could do worse for a long lost brother you know."

"Oh don't use the 'b' word, I can't think of him like that."

"How do you think of him?" Charley asked.

"I don't know," I replied, feeling confused. "Tell me what he's like, I didn't really chat to him."

"He's really nice. When we were in Venice, he couldn't do enough for me. He was so attentive, he was really keen on showing me around, pointing things out, and taking me places where the tourists don't normally go. He was so knowledgeable about its history, and also its future. I don't know if it was because of the report I was writing, but he went to great lengths to explain in minute detail the huge flood defence system that is being constructed to protect the city from flooding during high tides which he was really excited about. He is a very passionate person, but not in an intense way. Dandie I have to admit, I was really upset when I found out about him and Beth. At first I imagined that he wasn't that into her, that there was something between him and me, but seeing them together, how they interacted, how much they obviously cared about each other, I felt rather foolish."

"You really liked him didn't you?" I asked.

Charley drank some more wine.

"Yep, I did, still do. It was quite difficult having Beth staying, getting daily updates about how he was doing, hearing her stories of their life together. She mentioned Venice too, said she's been there with him several times. We shared experiences of Venice, but all the time I had to exclude Tom from my tales. We went to so many of the same places, she kept saying how funny it was that we'd both been to the same un touristy places. Then, when she realised that I'd met Tom in Venice, I think it all made sense to her. She wanted to know why I hadn't told her, I made out that I wasn't sure he was the same guy. She obviously trusts him because she didn't once seem jealous of our time spent together, quite the opposite. Once it was in the open that Tom and I had spent time together in Venice she seemed really pleased that we'd met and he'd been able to help me with my research."

We spent most of the evening talking about Tom, I was really eager to find out as much about him as I could. I left

Charley's around midnight, feeling much less troubled by Tom Bradley; I guess I was getting used to his existence.

The morning came around in a flash. I overslept and hurriedly got ready to meet Mum at the café. I was a bit late arriving and she was already sitting there waiting for me.

I have always pictured my mother as a tall, elegant lady, but strangely these last couple of weeks I have seen her in a different light. Somehow she seems much smaller, and vulnerable.

"Hello Dandie," she called out to me, smiling warmly.
I went over to her and she ordered me a coffee.
"Beautiful Dandie, how are you?" she asked.
"I'm fine Mum. More to the point, how are you?"
"Oh I'm just fine. Dad and I had a lovely few days away. We went to the Welsh coast and it was beautiful, the creeping sea mist was something to behold. I've never seen such an eerie and beautiful sight. Tell me your news, I hear whispers that there is a young man in your life," she seemed genuinely excited to hear more.

"Well, I have, I think."
"You think? What's he like?" Mum asked.
"Oh mum, he's lovely. He's tall, dark, handsome," we both laughed at the cliché.
"What's his name and what does he do?"
Standard parental questions really. I told her all about Ben and how I felt about him. She was so pleased and excited for me. Some time passed before I realised how cleverly she had drawn the conversation away from her and onto me.

"Mum, I'm worried about you, we all are," I said, reaching out for her hand, which she took and gently clasped.

"I'm ok Dandie, really I am," she paused and then continued, speaking slowly. "I think I should have told you all, prepared you. It's been very difficult for me Dandie. You cannot even begin to imagine the guilt and self-loathing I went through, am still going through. I thought about him and what I did often. Many sleepless nights I've had wishing things had been different. I felt so alone at the time as a young fifteen-year-old girl. I didn't really understand what was going on or the consequences. When you're pregnant you don't have long to make life-changing decisions.

I didn't even know I was pregnant until I was six months gone which is hard to believe, I know. I had less than three months to come to terms with the situation I was in. It was such a shock and is all a bit of a blur to me. I can't remember lots of details. I didn't feel at all in control about anything really.

I guess adoption was the best option under the circumstances, but it was never discussed. No one ever told me how I'd feel about it afterwards; the loss, the guilt, the feeling of failure. Also the feeling that I was incapable of making a sensible decision. That sense of uncertainty has plagued me all my adult life. I'm not sure I have ever felt confident that I have made a good decision.

As you grow older you learn to deal with these inner conflicts, studying counselling has helped me to understand how to deal with these feelings of self-doubt, but they're always there.

I didn't tell you for lots of complex reasons, but it wasn't just you, I didn't tell anyone, not even Lizzie. She still doesn't know."

Mum paused. I didn't say anything, just waited until she was ready to continue.

"When I heard about Tom, I cannot begin to explain how I felt. I was terrified. Terrified of you finding out and terrified he'd blame me. Terrified that he'd had an unhappy life. So many emotions which I'd hidden for such a long time resurfaced. I was exhausted, but I realised that I couldn't hide anymore. It was the least I could do to meet with him."

Again she paused, I could see how tired she was becoming, and tearful.

"He looks like Ash, don't you think? He has nice eyes too. It's so strange Dandie, he is so familiar to me, but I don't know him at all. How is that possible?" she continued.

"When we met he didn't hold any grudge against me. It seems he's had a very happy and stable life. He is close to his family and I like him... I feel very proud of him, am I allowed to say that?"

"Mum, there's one thing I must ask you." I said.

"Go on," Mum replied.

"The boy who made you pregnant, do you really have no idea who he is? Have you never wondered what he is up to?" I asked.

Mum didn't answer. I sat in silence with her for what seemed like forever. We drank our drinks and she even offered to get me a cake.

"Mum?" I said.

She looked at me and reached out for my hands across the table.

"Yes," she replied quietly.

"Yes what?" I asked, feeling slightly irritated.

"His name was Vincent Stead," she said quietly.

Chapter forty

Vincent Stead, the named seemed vaguely familiar but, I couldn't think why.

"Does Dad know?" I asked.

"No," she replied, sheepishly.

"Jeez Mum, how many other secrets do you have?" I asked crossly. I couldn't believe she had kept that from Dad.

"None," she replied quietly.

"Why, why didn't you tell Dad?" I demanded.

"Because that would have made him real."

"Of course he was real, he got you pregnant!" It was so weird, but Mum was acting like a teenager. It suddenly dawned on me that the last time she had spoken about this Vincent guy, she was a teenager, so maybe in some way that would explain her regression.

"Oh Dandie, it's so hard to explain. I didn't deal with the whole episode by pretending it hadn't happened, it was my way of coping. I'm sorry."

"Do you know what happened to him?" I asked.

"No, I never saw him again. Dandie, I've said too much, I need to go home now. I'm so sorry for everything." She leaned over and kissed me on the cheek.

"Mum, don't go, I don't want to part like this. Let me walk with you," I suggested.

"Ok," she replied and we left the Chocolate Café together arm in arm.

When we got to the crossroads we hugged each other goodbye.

"I love you Mum," I said to her.

"I love you too my darling, more than you could ever imagine."

I watched her as she walked away from me. She had always been so strong and dependable, I'd never seen this side of her before. I looked at her in a different light, and for maybe the first time, realised that she needed me as much as I needed her.

When she was out of sight I turned and headed home. Stuffed full of coffee and cakes, I didn't want any lunch. I still hadn't heard anything from Ben. I texted him asking him if he was free that evening. I didn't even think about it. As soon as I'd sent the text I questioned whether I should have, but in no time at all he texted back. Result! He was free and he wanted to see me. Yay! I really wanted to go to his place, but I couldn't very well invite myself round, so I invited him to mine. I had another date with Ben, I was happy.

I bought some food and wine on the way home, and as soon as I got back started cleaning the flat. I had my headphones in and the volume on full while I vacuumed, definitely the best way to do it: combining vacuuming with dancing, a kind of 'dance vac'. It made a mundane job fun anyway. I don't know what it is about vacuuming, but I find I get my most profound thoughts while doing it.

The name Vincent Stead sounded so familiar to me, but I couldn't think why. Was he someone I knew, worked with, a parent of one of my friends? It was rally bugging me, could I know the man who fathered Tom Bradley? I texted Charley asking if she had ever heard of a Vincent Stead? It is quite a memorable name after all. She texted back in the negative. I carried on vacuuming as Ben would be here soon, and I had to make the place nice for him.

Suddenly I stopped dead in my tracks and literally froze to the spot, vacuum in hand still going. I knew where I'd heard that name before. I dropped the vacuum and sat down on the sofa. Ben told me his dad was called Vincent. Ben's surname is Stead, so that makes his dad Vincent Stead! No, seriously, this couldn't be happening. This Tom Bradley was like some psychic mind warp! How could he keep popping up in my life like this, it wasn't fair. I had to quickly think, did this in any way make me and Ben genetically linked. I thought it over for a few seconds and came to the happy conclusion that it was ok; we were in no way blood related. Phew!

The doorbell rang, it was Ben. It was too soon, I wasn't ready. I let him in. He came up the stairs holding flowers. I was all a tizz, my mind was racing. The vacuum was still going and my headphones were still on although they were no longer attached to my head.

"I'm sorry, I'm just cleaning up, come in," I said nervously, not sure that the words even came out in the right order.
Ben came up to me, gave me a hug and kissed me on the lips. Under normal circumstances this would have been an extremely pleasant experience, but right now, all I could think about was that this gorgeous man in front of me is the son of the man who fathered Tom Bradley with my mother!

"Excuse the mess! Thanks for the flowers, they're lovely," I said, awkwardly.
"Dandie, are you ok?" he asked.
"Yes, sorry, I've just had some crazy news. I'll put the flowers in water."
Ben followed me through the living room.
"Shall I turn the vacuum off?" he asked.
"Oh, yes, please do," I stuttered.

I turned to look at Ben, and then just went over and hugged him.

"That's more like it. What's happened, what's the crazy news?" he asked, concerned.

"Oh, I wouldn't know where to begin," I replied, thinking, really where would I begin? I plonked down on the sofa, Ben sat down next to me. I poured us some wine as it seemed appropriate somehow.

"Do you know what I'd like to do right now?" I said.

"What do you want to do?" Ben asked.

"Get on a plane and fly to Venice!" I replied, laughing.

"Then let's do it!" Ben replied.

"Really?" I replied, slightly taken aback.

"Why not?" he said.

I smiled, momentarily feeling happy.

"I've already booked everything though," I said, suddenly panicked.

"Then I'd better book too."

I looked at him in awe. He was serious, he really wanted to come to Venice with me. I was dumbstruck, for the umpteenth time that day.

I got the laptop out and Ben went online and managed to get tickets for the same flights as mine. Result. I reached over and hugged him; I was immensely happy and impressed with his spontaneity. In two weeks' time we would be heading off for a week together in what promised to be the most beautiful of cities. After the excitement of booking our Venice trip we headed back to the sofa, drinks in hand.

"Ben, what are your mum and dad's names?" I asked.

"Vincent and Janet, why?" he replied.

"Oh, no reason," I replied, trying to sound casual. "Have they always lived around here?"

"Yes," Ben replied. "Although Dad didn't grow up here, I think he came here to go to uni, met Mum and stayed. When they split up he moved to London and she moved to the Lakes."

"How do you get on with your dad?"

"Not great, we've never really been his priority. I'd like to think that we're not very alike or have much in common," he said.

"How many siblings have you got?" I asked, and instantly regretted it.

"Three, Dandie, you know all this, I'm sure I've told you before. What's this all about?"

"Nothing, I just couldn't remember," I replied.

After the excitement of booking the trip I landed back down to earth with an almighty bump! It was more than likely that Ben's dad was also Tom Bradley's dad. Jeez, what am I to do now? Do I tell Ben – he wouldn't have a clue? It's almost certain that his dad has no idea that Mum became pregnant. What about Mum? How do I tell her that my new boyfriend's dad is Vincent?

This is one tricky situation. I could of course follow Mum's lead and not breathe a word to anyone, but then I'd be lying to all the people closest to me and I couldn't do that. Oh boy!

Chapter forty one

How I love Sunday mornings! Lying in bed with no plans and no time commitments. Relaxed and free. Admittedly waking up in my flat didn't have quite the romance of waking up at Ben's, but he was lying next to me asleep so I was happy. The sun was shining, *it's a nice day for a boat trip,* I thought.

As I began to wake up properly though, my thoughts drifted back to Vincent Stead. I could ignore the situation no longer. As I lay in bed my thoughts were swaying between relaxed boat trips and hassle-free Sundays (definitely my preferred line of thought) to spilling the beans on Vincent Stead.

I came to the unhappy conclusion that I was never going to have the relaxed care-free Sunday I hoped for unless I cleared the air and off loaded my knowledge. I made us both a coffee and brought them back to bed.

I gently woke Ben up. As I thought how I was going to approach the subject, I realised that this could potentially bring on the end of a beautiful friendship. I also realised that if I wasn't honest with him, there could be no true future for us.

"Wow, coffee brought to me in bed, what a treat," Ben said, as he sat up sleepily.
"Ben..." I began.
"Dandie," he replied, and reached out for a cuddle. I pushed him away, much to his surprise.

216

"Ben, there's something I need to tell you, and I don't know how to, so if you just listen and don't say anything, that might be best," Ben dutifully nodded, somewhat confused.

"This last week or so, some seriously weird things have happened – so weird in fact that it's totally blown my mind. I haven't mentioned anything of it to you, because, well I didn't really want to talk about it, and because it didn't have anything to do with you... or so I thought." I looked at him for reassurance but he was obediently keeping quiet, and still looked confused. I carried on.

"The long and short of it is, that I have a half-brother I didn't know existed, and your father is also his father." There I'd said it!

Ben spat out his coffee and burst out laughing.

"You're joking right?" he asked.

"Sorry, no," I replied.

Ben looked dumbstruck.

"Are we related?" he said, still very much in a state of confusion.

"No, most definitely not," I reassured him.

Ben didn't seem as upset about the revelation as I thought he would be, maybe because he didn't seem to have a very high opinion of Vincent, I don't know. Maybe he still thought that I wasn't being serious. He just sat up in bed and continued to drink his coffee. After a few minutes he said.

"You're one hundred per cent sure about this?"

"Yes, well ninety-nine per cent," I replied.

"Wow, what are the chances? Your mum and my dad, me and you. The attraction is consistent I'll say that."

Then a few minutes later, it seemed the penny dropped.

"I have a half-brother?" he announced, I nodded. "I've always wanted a brother."

Ben was certainly reacting to all this crazy linked up info much better than I had, I was impressed. He seemed to be taking it all in very matter-of-factly.

"What's he like, have you met him?" he asked.

"Only briefly, Ash had a good chat with him, he likes him."

"Our families are linked, wow." I could almost see the cogs of Ben's brain turning as he pieced together all this new information.

After an hour or so of explaining in detail everything that had gone on and all that I knew about Tom Bradley, I thought the best thing to do next was call Ash over. I rang him, he was of course thrilled to hear from me as usual.

"It's Sunday morning, this better be good!" and I invited him over for lunch. Ash never could turn down the offer of food, especially a big 'over the top' fry up. I was pleased that he and Ben were going to meet too.

Ash arrived eventually, and the worse for wear too. Turned out he'd had a major 'session' with his mates the previous night, and was suffering today. Considering how rough he felt I was flattered that he'd accepted my invitation, or was it simply the food that lured him over. Anyhow, he was here, and he was meeting Ben properly. I was so relieved, I knew they'd get along and it was important to me that they did too.

After lunch I bit the bullet and told Ash what Mum had told me about Vincent, and then told him about Vincent being Ben's dad. That bit didn't go down so well. Ash wasn't as mellow as Ben had been. Maybe I had been naïve in thinking that Ash would have reacted in a civilised, mature way. I had to admit that due to his delicate state, this may not have been the best time to divulge such information. Nevertheless, I was glad I'd told him and got it off my chest. What Ash chose to do now was up to him as I was well and truly tired of it all.

There was just one more thing to do and that was to tell mum about Vincent. Ash didn't hang around, he left to nurse his hangover. Maybe after he'd slept on it he'd be a bit calmer. It was a shame because Ben and Ash were getting along pretty well up until then.

Having upset Ash made me think back again to how simple and uncomplicated our lives had been before that fateful Tuesday. You think you know your family. You think that life just muddles along, you take things for granted and then out of nowhere everything is turned upside down and inside out, and you're left bemused trying to piece everything neatly back together again. I was so grateful that I found that money and was able to escape to Italy, boy did I need a change of scene.

Chapter forty two

Two weeks passed and Ben and I had not long arrived in Venice. Wow, it beats all expectations. The city was truly 'out of this world'. The sun was hot on my skin, the sky was blue, and the waves made by the passing boats lapped at the canal sides over my toes. As I looked around, my senses were overloaded with beauty, history and romance. It was such the right thing to do to go there and for Ben to be by my side really was unbelievable to me.

After 'that' Sunday, I'd been to see Mum and Dad and Mum had told Dad by then about Vincent. When I told them that I knew Vincent's son, Mum burst into tears.
"How can that be possible?" she kept saying.

Dad was, as always, her rock, ever supporting her. It was he who suggested contacting Vincent and telling him about Tom Bradley. So between the three families everything came out into the open.

Shock reverberated as you would imagine, and people reacted in their own peculiar ways. Rose, ever bitter and looking for a fight, flew off into a righteous rage condemning Vincent's behaviour. Ash eventually calmed down and soon moved on to focus on his band. Tom Bradley was overjoyed to have found not only his biological mother but also his father. Vincent was not practically interested, and acted as though he'd been duped. This I'd only heard third hand as I had still to meet Ben's family. Tom was recovering well with Beth loyally by his side.

It had been a month like no other, with coincidences so extraordinary I was still struggling to grasp them all. In truth I was glad to be out of it, I considered never leaving Venice – there were no cars with which to have crashes.

This is just the beginning of the rest of my life. If the last few weeks taught me anything, it's that nothing is certain, and everything can change in an instant.

Made in the USA
Charleston, SC
20 May 2016